LET SLE  E

I kept thinking how bizarre it was, how things got so out of hand: a stupid young man falls in love with a teacher. He gives her a cat. The teacher places the cat with a neighbor. The neighbor is unhappy. The teacher calls a friend to look the cat over. A thief breaks in and almost murders the friend who has absolutely nothing to do with anyone or anything in that apartment.

And now the lovesick student is murdered.

When I finally pulled myself away from my obsessive thoughts, I slipped into a very uncomfortable, agitated depression. Why did Bruce Chessler die? And what happened to the white cat?

No one had asked me these questions, but I couldn't let go. . . .

A
Cat of a
Different
Color

An Alice Nestleton Mystery

by
Lydia Adamson

A SIGNET BOOK

SIGNET
Published by the Penguin Group
Penguin Books USA Inc., 375 Hudson Street,
New York, New York 10014, U.S.A.
Penguin Books Ltd, 27 Wrights Lane,
London W8 5TZ, England
Penguin Books Australia Ltd, Ringwood,
Victoria, Australia
Penguin Books Canada Ltd, 2801 John Street,
Markham, Ontario, Canada L3R 1B4
Penguin Books (N.Z.) Ltd, 182-190 Wairau Road,
Auckland 10, New Zealand

Penguin Books Ltd, Registered Offices:
Harmondsworth, Middlesex, England

First published by Signet, an imprint of New American
Library, a division of Penguin Books USA Inc.

First Printing, May, 1991
10 9 8 7 6 5 4 3 2 1

The first chapter of this book previously appeared in
A Cat in the Manger.

REGISTERED TRADEMARK—MARCA REGISTRADA

Printed in the United States of America

PUBLISHER'S NOTE
This is a work of fiction. Names, characters, places, and
incidents either are the product of the author's imagi-
nation or are used fictitiously, and any resemblance to
actual persons, living or dead, events, or locales is en-
tirely coincidental.

BOOKS ARE AVAILABLE AT QUANTITY DISCOUNTS WHEN USED
TO PROMOTE PRODUCTS OR SERVICES. FOR INFORMATION
PLEASE WRITE TO PREMIUM MARKETING DIVISION, PENGUIN BOOKS
USA INC., 375 HUDSON STREET, NEW YORK, NEW YORK 10014.

A
CAT OF A
DIFFERENT
COLOR

1

The woman, whose name was Francesca Tosques—she was vaguely attached to the Italian legation—had told me before I started the cat-sitting assignment that Geronimo was a lovely cat but he had some peculiarities.

"Don't go near the fireplace," she said mysteriously. "Fine!" I replied. Francesca was going to be away for three days: Sunday, Monday, and Tuesday. All I had to do was go up to her large old apartment on West End Avenue and Ninety-seventh Street in Manhattan . . . feed Geronimo . . . talk to Geronimo . . . kill some time. That's all. A very good assignment as these things go.

I arrived on Sunday at three in the afternoon, walking all the way from my East Twenty-sixth Street apartment, through the park. It was hot outside but the apartment was cool without air conditioning, utilizing only one large slow ceiling fan. The view from the apartment was spectacular: out over the Hudson to Jersey, or north up the Hudson, or downtown. Pick a window, pick a view. She had left me twenty-three notes on the dining-room table, complicating the simplest procedures. But I was used to that.

As for Geronimo—I was expecting a Balinese or a Cornish Rex or some other exotic feline, but when I finally met him—he was lying on the Formica kitchen table—well, Geronimo was simply an old-fashioned black alley cat. You couldn't call him anything else. He was big and brawny and ugly, with scars up and down his flanks, and he walked, when he did walk, like alley cats do—as if he had some kind of testicular problem, to put it kindly.

That first day, I stayed in the apartment about an hour, talking to Geronimo, who really wasn't listening. After eating, he had gone back to the Formica table and I had to almost shout to get my points across. I joshed him, telling him that I was a famous actress, a famous sleuth, and above all, a famous cat sitter, and I'd be damned if he was going to be standoffish. I just wouldn't tolerate it.

On the third day, we weren't any friendlier; it was live and let live. Anyway, on that third and last day of the assignment, Geronimo was beginning to irritate me. And my pride was hurt. Everyone always said I had a magical way with cats. Ask my own cats—Bushy and Pancho. They'll tell anyone. So it started to bother me about what his mistress had told me—that I should not go near the fireplace. Very strange. The fireplace was an old large one, set in the north wall of the apartment. It was obviously a working fireplace but it was also obvious that it hadn't been used in a long time. I had kept away from it because of what she had told me and because it was in a far part of the apartment. I mean, one really had to want to go there to end up there. So I sat and stewed at the living-room table, staring at Geronimo, who was staring at me from the kitchen table. Instead of a forty-one-year-old woman, I was thinking like a twelve-year-old adolescent. Something had been denied me. Authority had spoken. It was necessary to subvert authority. It was a decidedly adolescent impulse.

I got up slowly, theatrically, elegantly, and sauntered over to the fireplace. Reaching it, I placed one hand gently on the mantelpiece and smiled.

A moment later a blur seemed to explode across the room. And then I felt a short intense pain in the thumb of the hand resting on the fireplace.

Startled, I looked down. Geronimo was standing there. He had flown across the room and bitten me. Can you imagine that?

Then the cat turned and sauntered back toward the kitchen table, very much the macho alley cat.

In a state of semishock from the attack, I stumbled into the bathroom and let running cold water clean the small wound. Geronimo stared at me from his kitchen table, bored, inferring that I had been duly warned and that since I had obviously wanted to play with fire, it was simple justice that I got burnt.

After I washed and dressed the wound I felt exhausted. I walked into Francesca Tosques' bedroom and lay down on the bed, closing my eyes and flicking on the radio. The station was set on 1010 WINS—news all the time.

I lay there wondering why Geronimo attacked people who stood in front of the fireplace. It was very perplexing. I must have dozed off and then awakened with a start. My mouth was dry. A bad dream? No. A name on the radio was being repeated, and I knew the name. The announcer was saying that one of the last famous Greenwich Village bohemians was dead. Arkavy Reynolds had been shot to death on Jane Street. Reynolds, the announcer said, was a well-known denizen of the lower Manhattan theatrical scene. He was a producer, publisher of a theatrical scandal sheet which he hawked himself from coffee shop to coffee shop, and one of those outrageous individuals who at one time were so much a part of bohemian life in New York. The announcer ended with the comment that the police were investigating the murder but had no leads or witnesses at this time.

Poor Arkavy! I had bumped into him often over the years and we always chatted, or rather I listened to his monologue. He was a huge fat man who seemed to roll down the street. In all seasons he wore the same outfit: a cabdriver's hat, white shirt and flamboyant tie, vest, farmer's overalls with shoulder straps, and construction-worker shoes. Of course, he was quite mad. Rumor had it he came from a wealthy family. He was always looking for space to perform some play far off-off Broadway. He was always talking about some brilliant new playwright whom no one had ever heard of. And his newsletters were often about people that simply didn't exist. Each issue of his newsletter also carried reviews written by him, which were filled with typographical excesses—he loved asterisks and exclamation marks and dots and dashes.

I got up from the bed and walked into the kitchen. There was Geronimo. He no longer interested me at all. I ignored him. I opened and closed the refrigerator a few times absentmindedly, thinking of Arkavy, trying to remember the exact time I had last seen him. It might have been on East Fourth Street and First Avenue one night in the fall of 1989. I was going to a dramatic reading by an East German woman. Yes, it might have been then.

I left the kitchen and walked back into the living room, where I fell wearily into a chair. My wound was beginning to throb. Geronimo was still looking at me. It dawned on me, right then, that if Arkavy and Geronimo had by chance met, they might have become the best of friends. After all, poor Arkavy was a man who had spent his life looking to be bitten.

2

It was ten o'clock in the morning. I was standing in front of the public school on Eighty-first Street and Madison Avenue, staring across the street at the Frank E. Campbell funeral home, where poor Arkavy Reynolds' body could be viewed in the coffin before burial. The public had been invited to pay their last respects. Well, that was what I intended to do. He had been perpetually a fresh breath of lunatic air in the New York theatrical world. Time had passed him by . . . the New York theater was now show biz or high finance—all aspects of it—and I owed it to him to stare at his corpse.

The *Times* printed a small article about him in the theatrical section, not the obituary section. The reporter had called it just another senseless New York tragedy. Arkavy, it seems, had fought with a panhandler at Sheridan Square on the morning of his death. The police speculated that the panhandler got a weapon, went looking for Arkavy, found him on Jane Street, and shot him five times in the chest. The reporter said Arkavy Reynolds' last-known residence was a seamen's shelter down near South Street.

And then the article went on to recount some of the more colorful "Arkavy" stories—like his predilection for taking cabs and then paying the meter with off-off-Broadway theater tickets from shows that had closed years ago.

Why didn't I just cross the street and walk inside the funeral parlor? Why was I hesitating? I don't know, but I dawdled there for the longest time. The morning was sunny and warm but without humidity, and there was a gentle early-August breeze blowing up Madison Avenue.

I waited until I saw a group of people who might be theater folk enter the funeral parlor and then I crossed quickly against the light and went in on their heels. I had my long gray-gold hair pulled up in a bun and I was wearing leather sandals and a long loose white dress with marigolds on it.

Inside was all marble and gentility. A well-dressed man with a carnation inquired as to the name of the deceased and, once given, pointed me to the stairs. I walked up swiftly and found the room.

Arkavy Reynolds was laid out in a brass coffin. There were only eight or nine people in the room, moving awkwardly from wall to wall. Great bunches of flowers were present, still wrapped in their cellophane delivery shrouds.

I walked to the coffin, close up, and stared down. Arkavy was lying there in some sort of garment. He had lost weight in death. He had little hair on his head, which surprised me, but then again, I had never seen him in life without his hat. The moment I looked at him, I realized how stupid and sentimental I had been in coming. Arkavy would have found it too funny for words.

"A nice man," I heard someone say very close to me.

I turned. An old woman with a pink straw hat was standing with the help of a cane and looking past the coffin at the wall.

"A very nice man," she repeated, and then added, "and he was so good to his mother before she died. Did you know his mother?"

I shook my head.

"Did you know his family is from Albany?" she asked.

"No."

"Yes, Albany," she affirmed, smiled, and then hobbled away. I looked at the coffin again. It was all too sad. Who knows what dreams Arkavy had when he arrived in New York all those years ago from Albany . . . thirsting for the theatrical life, which was then the bohemian life . . . for beauty and truth through artifice . . . for *épater la bourgeoisie*. Did he really think New York would be like the Paris of Baudelaire? The fool. I turned away and walked quickly out of the viewing room to the stairs.

I hadn't gone three steps down when a young man walking up loomed in front of me and barred my path.

He had thick black curly hair and equally thick eyebrows lying over very radiant blue eyes. He was wearing the ugliest Hawaiian sport shirt I had ever seen, hanging loose over his belt. My first thought was: How did they let him in?

He grinned at me and didn't move aside. He said: "Beneath this rock there doth lie all the beauty that could ever die."

I stared dumbly at him. Something about him was very familiar.

"Ben Jonson," he said, identifying the quote.

And then I uttered a long, exasperated groan. Of course I knew him. What bloody bad luck! I had just started teaching a course in the second summer session at the New School. The class had met only once so far. And this young man had already become a pain in the posterior. A severe pain. It was just the introductory session of the course, so I had thrown out to the class a childish bone—what came into their minds when the word "theater" was mentioned. This young man, the one now blocking my exit, had leapt up and launched into a long violent diatribe about the American theater, quoting and approving and expanding Brecht's comment that Broadway was simply one segment of the international drug trade. He had immediately alienated all the other students to such a degree that they started yelling at him . . . and my fine gentle introductory session had turned into a shambles.

"What are you doing here?" I asked him.

"Paying my respects to a madman, Professor, just like you."

"May I pass?" I asked, my voice growing angry.

He stepped aside and bowed low in an Elizabethan flourish, his grotesque shirt billowing, showing the lean muscular stomach underneath.

"May I introduce myself?" he asked, grinning.

"No need," I replied, and walked swiftly down the stairs and out of the building.

Once outside, on Madison Avenue, I breathed deeply. What a fiasco! I wanted very much to be back in my apartment with Bushy and Pancho. I wanted very much to be far away from that sad dead man and that obnoxious young man. So I took a cab home.

3

One cannot control one's students. At least I never could. Worse, I inspire them, always, the wrong way.

"Is it true that most actors are lousy lovers?"

I stared at the heavyset girl in the second row who had asked me that question. Was she serious? Was it a serious question?

I tried not to make a face, but I was disgusted with the question. This was a summer-school course at the prestigious New School for Social Research—an elite institution. It was supposed to be a serious course; about the theater and the actress in New York City . . . how they interact . . . how each enlightens, cripples, and modifies the other.

But all I had gotten during the first three sessions was a series of stupid questions. In fact, there were only six sessions left. When would I gain control of the course? When would I be able to move the students to a higher level? I had taught a few classes in the past . . . in acting schools . . . and some at City College. Some of them had turned out to be memorable. A professor at City College once told me that my lecture on *Waiting for Godot* was the best and most exciting piece of Beckett analysis he had ever heard. I had brought a homeless woman to the class to show my students that Beckett's portrayal of tramps had nothing to do with any reality whatsoever . . . that the tramps in Beckett's great play were in disguise. And then, with the class's participation, I began to peel off the disguise . . . to discover who those tramps really were. Where had they worked? What were their medical problems? What country were they from? The class was in an uproar. It was the most remarkable explosion of good chemistry I had ever experienced. But that was then. And the times were different. And the milieu was different. And perhaps I was different. None of that good chemistry had emerged so far in the New School class.

Maybe it was futile, I thought, as I also thought of a way to answer the lousy-lover question. I had obtained this teaching job, in fact, only because of a stupid article about me buried in the theater section of the Sunday *New York Times.* So maybe they expected me to field stupid questions. Anyway, the opening paragraph of that article had read:

At forty-one, Alice Nestleton is still an unknown to the general public, but in the inner circle of the New York theater world her recent interpretation of the Nurse in a Portobello production of *Romeo and Juliet* in Montreal is considered a brilliant dramaturgical exploration. In addition, Miss Nestleton has a very interesting hidden life—crime. She has recently received a commendation from the Nassau County Police Department for her help in solving several grisly murders on the North Shore of Long Island, which took her into the rarefied atmosphere of the thoroughbred-horse world.

The article then went on to briefly document the roles I had played in the past and to discuss my interpretation of the role of the Nurse.

Let's be honest. It was that damn article that got me the job and, believe me, what the New School pays buys a lot of cat food.

"I haven't had too many lovers who were actors," I said to the class, "so I really can't judge them. The ones I did have were medium-rare."

Laughter in the class. The air conditioning was breaking down again. One of the students had opened the window in the rear; a sticky, hot, and humid August air seemed to envelop us. It was a night class. The students worked during the day. They were paying their hard-earned money for insights into the life of the actress in New York, but they hadn't given me a chance yet to explore it with them. They were fixated on bizarre things: who did I sleep with? . . . where did I buy my clothes? . . . how did I support myself between parts? None of them really relevant to *the* problem, which was the structure of the theater itself and how it destroys the actress like a sausage-making machine.

I stole a glance at the right rear of the classroom. That was where my nemesis always sat—the young man in the Hawaiian sport shirt who had accosted me in the funeral parlor. His classroom behavior had continued to be unbelievable. I seemed to irritate him severely. I seemed to lack the dedication he required. I seemed to be his ogre of a decaying theatrical class. He challenged. He emoted. He screamed. He wept. He was wearisome. But sometimes he looked at me with such a strange, fierce look, I had the feeling that he and he alone in the class knew I was a very good teacher when the time and place were right. And always, from the first moment he walked into class, I felt that he was watching me, studying me, waiting to pounce on me, and wanting very much to anticipate the things I would say and the movements I would make.

His seat was empty! Thank God! Maybe he had withdrawn from the course. It was a cheering thought.

I looked at my watch. Eight-thirty-two. The class was supposed to run until nine.

How does one abort a class? Would the students be happy? Or would they feel cheated?

A middle-aged woman with startlingly gray hair raised her hand. I acknowledged her.

"I want you to address Portobello's concept of Shakespeare."

God bless you, lady, I thought. I was about to do it, but suddenly I became weary . . . very weary. I wanted to go home . . . I wanted to feed my cats.

I smiled at her. "Why don't we quit early tonight, and I'll start the next class with Portobello." I was suggesting, asking, begging.

They leapt at the chance. Without another word, they gathered their packages, half-eaten sandwiches, carryalls, and paperbacks. They were as happy to leave as I.

One girl remained as the others flew out. She was an actress. I just knew it. I couldn't handle her worshipful gaze, as if I had truly "made it." I hadn't. My income was still primarily from cat-sitting, from playing games with oftentimes borderline psychotic felines like the beloved Geronimo.

"At least," she said, "that idiot didn't show up."

She was wearing a tank top. She had short brown hair and incredibly intense green eyes.

"That's for sure," I replied, smiling, thinking of the blessed absence of that young man who had tormented me maliciously during the first few sessions. Then the girl became shy and said nothing. An awkward minute passed. Then two minutes. Finally, she left.

I waited sixty seconds and was starting to exit when two men entered the classroom. They didn't come all the way inside, hovering near the door and smiling at me. They introduced themselves. Cops. Detectives Felix and Proctor. They were attached to some task force with an incredibly bizarre bureaucratic name. Young men, clean-cut, vacant eyes.

"You are Alice Nestleton?" the one named Proctor asked.

"Yes." I had no idea what they wanted.

They laid out on my desk in a scattered pattern about twenty photographs. I looked at them. In most of them the backdrop was the inside of the Frank E. Campbell Funeral Home, where Arkavy Reynolds had laid in state.

"You took pictures at the funeral home? Why?" I was astonished.

"Arkavy Reynolds was a good snitch. An informer. He helped us. We helped him. We don't like it when one of our own gets blown apart by a semiautomatic twenty-five-caliber Beretta in broad daylight."

Arkavy a police informer? My God! It was too bizarre. What did he inform about? Dressing-room sex at the Public Theater?

The one called Felix, who was wearing an old-fashioned button-down shirt, asked me to go over the photos. I identified myself. I identified the obnoxious student. I identified a few other people—theater people—whom I hadn't seen in the funeral parlor because they arrived earlier or later than my visit. The detectives made notes on the backs of the photographs I had identified.

"What time was he murdered?" I asked.

"Late morning," Proctor answered.

"Were there any witnesses? Do you have any suspects?"

"We're working on it, lady," Felix answered testily.

"Did you check out his room? I think he lived in a seamen's shelter downtown."

"We know where he lived."

"Did you check out his coffee shops? He

used to go to one on Fifth, just east of Second and the Polish coffee shop on Tompkins Square Park."

"We know where he hung out," Proctor replied.

I was about to ask another question when Felix exploded: "What the hell is going on here? Are you a cop? Who is interrogating who?"

"No one is interrogating anyone," I replied softly, then let the dust settle before I asked another perfectly plausible question.

"Why would the murderer show up at the wake?" I asked.

"You never know," Detective Felix said, then gathered up the photographs, thanked me, and left. I had the sense that the two men were oddly foreign . . . like they were from Belgium or some place like that.

One of them stuck his head back through the door. "By the way, we found you because one of the ushers at the funeral home saw you once in an off-Broadway show. He said you were very good, but he didn't remember the name of the play."

It was almost ten when I finally began climbing the five flights of stairs to my apartment. I was carrying a large bag of groceries, which included various tidbits for my Maine coon cat, Bushy, and my tailless ASPCA contribution, Pancho.

The hallway was stifling. But there was only one more landing to go. The stairs were so familiar that I had lost my sense of climbing and thought only of the cats waiting for me . . . waiting in the darkness . . . each doing his own thing. Bushy was probably stretched out on the sofa, one eye open, his stomach purring softly at the thought of the coming food. Pancho was probably just finishing one of his lunatic dashes from cabinet to cabinet in the kitchen, running from shadowy enemies.

In fact, I was so wrapped up in the cats, I never saw the figure sitting at the top of the landing until he said: "Happy Birthday, Professor."

I froze in fear—staring through the dim light.

"Happy Birthday, Professor," the voice repeated in a mocking tone.

The outline of a man, a young man, was sitting calmly.

Next to him on the stairs was a large carton wrapped in paper, with ribbons hanging from it.

A thief? A rapist? A psychotic derelict? I didn't know. I wanted to run, but my feet remained rooted.

My grocery bag, I thought. I can fling my bag at him and run down the steps. But I didn't.

"Who are you? How did you get in? What do you want?"

"Theater!" he shouted dramatically.

Oh, God! My fear abated for the first time. It was my nemesis: the obnoxious student from the back of the class who had not showed up for the most recent lessons, thankfully—the same one I had met in the funeral parlor.

"What are you doing here?" I yelled, anger replacing the initial fear . . . anger at his arrogance and stupidity and craziness. I was so weary of him.

"I brought you a birthday present," he replied.

"It's not my birthday."

The young man stood up for the first time. Even in the bad light I could see that he was wearing one of his ghastly loud sport shirts. He was taller than I had remembered, and older. He had a small blunt nose and his large eyes seemed green in the hallway—not blue. His skin was very white.

I was tired. I was angry. I snapped at him: "Please move aside with your box and let me get into my apartment."

I had spoken to him like I was a kindergarten teacher and he was a recalcitrant tot.

He didn't move. He didn't speak.

The clock was ticking. Tick-tock. His shirt was drenched with sweat; large stains moved from his arms to the center of the fabric.

Then he moved quickly, down the steps, toward me—so quickly I couldn't respond at all.

At the last moment he sidestepped, just brushing me with his face, whispering: "I love you."

And then he was gone to the next landing below. His steps were like a receding train . . . quicker and lighter in the distance.

"Your box," I yelled out after him, pointing

at the item he had left behind on the top of the landing.

But it was too late. He was gone.

Oh, God, I thought. All I needed now was a crazy student who had fallen in love with me. But there was a more immediate problem. I had to open my apartment door with an extra large package in addition to my shopping bag—without the cats getting out.

I reached the top landing and began to push the large birthday box toward the door of my apartment with my foot.

Halfway there the box began to vibrate furiously, ribbons flapping and unraveling.

I stepped back startled.

Before I could do anything, the box turned over on its side.

Out leapt a very large and very beautiful snow-white cat with a black-spotted face and a black-spotted rump.

The cat leapt onto the banister and stood there—eyeing me malevolently.

4

I stared at the creature from the box with a kind of shocked disbelief.

It was one of the most beautiful cats that ever hissed at me. My first thought, as I moved toward it slowly, was that it was an Abyssinian; it had that long-legged cougar look which so distinguished the breed.

But then I realized my identification was nonsense. There is no such thing as a white Abyssinian. And, to make matters even more absurd, this cat, now elongated against the banister as if it was about to spring, had black spots on face and rump.

"Now, be reasonable, Clara," I said to her as I inched my way forward, not having the faintest idea why I called her Clara. She wasn't impressed. When I was about ten inches away, she leapt lightly off the banister and came to a stop in front of my door. She sat and stared at me.

Inside my apartment, my cats were scurrying. I could hear them through the door. Reality dawned on me. I could not take Clara into the apartment with my own cats. It was too dangerous . . . too problematic—God knows what would happen!

I stood still and silently cursed that idiotic young man who had left me Clara. Was this the way he expressed his adolescent love? God help me if he falls out of love, I thought—he'll deposit a real cougar on the stairs, gift-wrapped also.

What were my options? Well, I could just leave the cat in the hallway and hope that it would wander to a different floor and some-one kindly would give it a home. Or I could take it to an animal shelter. But that was dangerous—cats in shelters are two cans of tuna fish away from the gas chamber. No, Clara couldn't go there.

Clara stared at me. I stared at Clara. The solution was obvious. Board Clara out until the next class at the New School, when I could demand that the retarded Lothario re-trieve his poor cat.

But with whom could I board her? I knew only one person close by . . . only one person well enough for me to have the audacity to ask.

I walked quickly down the hallway to the last door on the left and knocked, calling out: "Mrs. Oshrin. It's me, Alice Nestleton. It's all right. It's me." I had to talk loud because Mrs. Oshrin was a bit hard of hearing. She opened the door. She was a very stout woman, about sixty-five, a retired teacher. We always went shopping together on Saturday mornings, to the farmers' market at Union Square Park. For some reason she called me Alice and I called her Mrs. Oshrin. Maybe she intimi-dated me a bit. She used to be a minor

Democratic-party official and she still talked incessantly about city politics when given the chance.

"What is the matter?" she asked, frightened. She always thought something was the matter. I pointed down the hallway, where the white cat still sat.

"Who is that?" Mrs. Oshrin asked. As if it were a distant relative who had suddenly arrived and was about to ask a favor. She was right.

"Her name is Clara," I said.

"Clara," Mrs. Oshrin repeated, as if the name rang a bell in her memory.

"Yes, Clara, and she needs a home for just a day or two."

My voice was pleading. Mrs. Oshrin could never withstand my needs. She was a very nice lady. She stared out down the hallway again.

"But what do I do? I never had a cat."

That was all I needed. I rushed to my shopping bag, took out a can of cat food, ran into Mrs. Oshrin's apartment, opened it, strolled down the hallway to Clara so she could get a whiff, then carried the can back to Mrs. Oshrin's apartment. I left the door open and placed the can about ten feet inside.

Then Mrs. Oshrin and I sat down on her sofa. We waited. We waited. We chatted.

Then we saw one white ear. Then a black-and-white nose. Then a long lean body flitted through the doorway.

Clara was inside. We beamed at each other. Mrs. Oshrin watched Clara inspect the food and then walk regally away. The cat was beginning to explore.

"Why doesn't she eat the food?" Mrs. Oshrin asked.

"She will," I said.

We watched.

"My sister had a cat," Mrs. Oshrin noted.

I realized that Mrs. Oshrin and I were about to lapse into one of our constant Pinteresque dialogues that went on and on and nowhere at all. Usually I enjoyed them, but now I wanted to feed my poor cats.

"Everything will be all right, Mrs. Oshrin. Just talk to her once in a while. I'll call you tomorrow." And then I was gone, leaving the bewildered woman with a new companion.

I called Mrs. Oshrin five times the next day to make sure she and Clara were getting along. Mrs. Oshrin did not seem to be enjoying the stranger but she was calm, stoic, and asked me only three or four times when I would get Clara out. Soon, I said, soon.

I discussed the problem with Bushy, my Maine coon cat. He was noncommittal. As for Pancho, he never stayed still long enough to listen.

As the hours passed and I came closer to my class, my anger toward that young man grew to truly monumental proportions. I envisioned an almost Elizabethan scene of vengeance and condemnation. Then I mellowed somewhat—after all, the young man was in love with a forty-one-year-old actress with long golden-gray hair and a reputation for dramatic innovation—me. I was, to be truthful, just a bit vain. And it had been a long time since I had elicited that kind of passion from anyone. Besides, that kind of crazy young man was what kept the theater alive. No wonder he had gone to Arkavy Reynolds' funeral. The young Arkavy had been a bohemian firebrand. Theater or death! It wasn't a game. It wasn't an art. It wasn't a pastime for speculators or dilettantes. The theater was life itself. Did *I* still have any of that commitment?

I arrived at the class earlier than usual and sat at my desk doodling. The students straggled in. The heavyset woman who had asked about Portobello smiled at me. I nodded to her, signifying that yes, indeed, I would deal with her inquiries in this class, this evening.

The young man never arrived. As I was giving my disjointed lecture, I kept anticipating the door opening and a lovesick young man with a ghastly sport shirt flitting in.

Thirty minutes before the class was about to end I abandoned the lecture, which they were all obviously finding boring, and asked point-blank if anyone in the class knew the missing young man who wore loud sport shirts and wisecracked all the time. Did anyone know his name?

The students looked at each other. They were perplexed. Curious. This was the New School. In Manhattan. No one asked or gave names in a formal sense. No one called the roll. At most, one student would say to another, "I'm Jo Anne. Hi." As for me, I had been given a list of the names of all the students who had signed up for the course—but I had discarded it immediately.

"He left something in the classroom," I told the class, a gentle half-lie. No one in the seats in front of me uttered a word. I dismissed them early and angrily.

As I was gathering my things from off the desk, that ingenue in the tank top said: "He told me his name was Bruce. He asked me to have a cup of coffee with him after the first class. I said no."

I smiled my thanks. She waited to see if I was willing to talk theater with her. Then, seeing that my thoughts were elsewhere, she left. My thoughts were indeed elsewhere. The name Bruce didn't help me. What was I going to do with poor Mrs. Oshrin?

5

There was a new line on my face, on the left side, going from the edge of the mouth to the chin. It was ever so gentle and straight—but it was there.

"You are getting old, Alice Nestleton. And you are getting quirkier. And you are . . ."

I stopped speaking to myself in the mirror and concentrated on my brushing. Pancho was on the high bookcase, his rust-colored whiskers quivering just a bit, and his gaunt gray body with the scar on one side in a state of extreme alert for the unseen furies which were always chasing him. I raised the brush slowly and, in the mirror, watched his eyes follow the movement.

It was ten o'clock in the morning. I had overslept. Several times during the night I had woken with a start from the same nightmare. In the dream I was lying in a coffin in the Frank E. Campbell Funeral Home on Madison Avenue and Arkavy Reynolds was paying his last respects to my body. But then my grandmother appeared and she and Arkavy got into a terrible row. And I kept waking up to stop their fighting. It was not just arguing—it was something horrible they were doing to each other. Each time I awoke, my heart was beating fast. But now the fear was gone. For the first time in days there was a cool breeze moving through my apartment; a promise of the autumn soon to come.

When I finished brushing, I made a cup of coffee and took it into the living room. Bushy was snoozing on the sofa, his head lying on a script. I removed the thin folder gently, but it woke him. He looked up at me, hurt, and then leapt to the floor to continue his nap on the carpet, groaning a bit at my incredible lapse of manners.

The script itself was only thirty pages long and bound into a strange-colored binder, a dull yellow. It had been sent to me by an old friend who taught at Boston University but who spent all his money and time on theatrical productions in the New England area. We had only one thing in common—we both craved, sought for, aspired to theatrical pieces that were far outside the mainstream. We both wanted to explore the reality of the stage and the players and the relation of both to "what there is"—so we were both perpetually frustrated. I held the dull yellow binder in my hand with a kind of weariness. After all, I knew that the theater was so tyrannized by normalcy that even a Brecht play was not considered avant-garde.

My Medaglia d'Oro instant coffee, however, was black and sweet and bracing, and the breeze in the living room was truly delightful, so I opened the stiff front cover and began to read.

I burst out laughing when I read the title page: *Rats: An Alternative to Cats.*

The "Cats," of course, being the long-running Broadway musical of that name.

It wasn't really a script. It was a discussion of a performance. There are seven rats in the cast, part of an extended family which lives beneath the theater where *Cats* is playing.

The rats speak a kind of fractured Shakespearean English and they are hopelessly violent, oversexed, venal, and lunatic—a kind of murderous Marx Brothers.

A new litter is born, and this new litter, which lives offstage in large boxes among the audience, develops a decided taste for human flesh, particularly for the actors and actresses who play the cats in the musical of the same name.

It was a delicious, bizarre, very funny dramatic mess and I was just getting deep into the gory theatrics when I heard someone knocking.

At first I thought it was someone on the street. But no, someone was at my door. I approached cautiously and said hello through the wood.

"It's me, Alice," said the voice. Mrs. Oshrin.

I opened the door. She was standing there in a housedress, her arms folded, looking very clumsy and gloomy.

The sight of her unnerved me. I had forgotten all about Clara, the white cat, while reading the script.

Mrs. Oshrin marched in and sat down on the sofa. She seemed to be very upset but trying to control herself. I knew there was trouble because she was wearing a very bright and new housedress. That was one of Mrs. Oshrin's sure signals that things were not going well with her. Another sure signal was the fact that she didn't look around my living room with her usual critical stare. Mrs. Oshrin didn't like my living room. The furniture didn't bother her. She liked the large French sofa I had bought at Pierre Deux in the Village when I was temporarily affluent. She liked the long, narrow oak dining room table. She liked my three cane chairs near the window and my beat-up coffee table. What she never liked was the clutter. But there was nothing I could do about that. My kitchen was small. My bedroom smaller. The long, very narrow hall which ran the length of my apartment had to be kept clear if it was to remain passable. So everything ended up in my living room. I truly lived in my living room, and the clutter was just too much for her. Oh, there was no question Mrs. Oshrin was out of sorts.

"Can I get you some coffee?" I asked.

"No, thank you."

I sat down on the sofa next to her.

"Is Clara giving you any trouble?" I asked.

There was no answer.

"I was going to bring you some more cat food this afternoon," I said.

There was no answer. I could see that she was glaring at poor Bushy.

"Alice," she finally said in a very peculiar voice, "I am going to visit my sister in Connecticut."

"Well, that's nice," I replied happily.

She reached into her housedress and retrieved a single key attached to a rather large piece of wood.

Now she was staring at the ceiling. Poor Mrs. Oshrin; by this time I had surmised the visit had to do with Clara. Once again I silently cursed that young man who had caused all these problems.

"And when I come back," she said firmly, "I would like very much if that cat was in its new home."

"Of course, Mrs. Oshrin," I said quickly. It was obvious that Clara was ruining our relationship.

"Has she been much bother?" I asked.

Mrs. Oshrin didn't answer. She stood up, smoothed her housedress, gave me the key, smiled kindly, and just walked out, not letting me know what kind of horrendous behavior Clara had exhibited.

That killed my day. If she would be back in a day or two, I had to find someplace else for Clara to reside, very quickly.

In the next ten hours I must have made about fifty phone calls. The range and variety of excuses why these people could not board orphan Clara were mind-boggling. But they all said no. No matter how endearingly

I described Clara, the answer was the same—
no.

It was around ten o'clock in the evening
that I finally made an intelligent move. I
called John Cerise. Now, John has absolutely
nothing to do with the theater. He's a cat
man, pure and simple. In fact, he was always
a source of cat-sitting assignments for me.
We met years ago when I first started cat-
sitting for a rich lady on Central Park West
whose passion was English short-hairs. Cerise was a cat-show judge and breeder who
lived somewhere in New Jersey. He is a gentle, knowledgeable man, now in his sixties,
whose love for cats is proverbial. We rarely
speak to each other more than two or three
times a year, but there is a genuine affection
between us, and he has a special spot in his
heart for crazed Pancho, who, he once said,
is a reincarnation of one of Napoleon's mar-
shals.

What made me think of John Cerise was
the fact that when I first saw Clara I had
thought she was an Abyssinian, and Cerise,
I knew, was breeding Abyssinians. He loved
Abys, as he called them and, while normally
a quiet man, would immediately discourse on
them if given the chance. About how they are
the true descendants of the sacred cats of ancient Egypt. About how they are the only
breed with a close wild relative still extant—
the North African desert cat, *Felis libyca*.
About their wild looks but gentle affectionate
nature. About how difficult they are to breed.
About the strange fact that they produce pre-

dominantly male litters. About what excellent swimmers they are because they actually like water. And on and on.

I didn't lie to him when I called. But I didn't quite tell him the truth either. I concocted a gentle, imaginative story. There was this very strange-looking Abyssinian staying at a friend's apartment. Could he stop over and check it out, and if he didn't want it, recommend someone who would like it? I told him nothing about the deranged romanticism which had brought the cat to me and Mrs. Oshrin. He agreed. He laughingly asked for clarification of my phrase "a strange-looking Abyssinian." I got off the phone fast.

He arrived at seven-thirty the next morning. It was very good to see him again. He was wearing one of those elegant white linen suits, a blue silk tie, and a lighter blue silk shirt. His still-black hair was slicked back. John Cerise always looked exotic—an ageless relic from another time and another place. It was fitting he was a cat man. He seemed to be perfectly and easily androgynous. He reeked of a kind of cool sensuality which was quite pleasing to watch, although one could rarely identify the object of his passion.

We walked down the hallway to Mrs. Oshrin's. I opened the door with her key and stepped inside, closing the door behind us.

"She's white," I whispered as we waited in the living room for Clara to appear. Why was I whispering?

"White?" John asked, astonished.

I nodded. Clara did not appear.

"Maybe she's in the bedroom," I said. We walked into Mrs. Oshrin's bedroom. Clara wasn't there either.

She wasn't in the kitchen. She wasn't in the closets. She wasn't under anything.

We were puzzled.

"Make some noise," John suggested.

I banged one of Mrs. Oshrin's bronze bric-a-brac against a table leg. It made a dull thudding noise. Clara was not interested.

"The bathroom," John said.

We walked there quickly and found Clara in the bathtub, staring malevolently at a slow drip from the bath faucet. Our presence seemed to make absolutely no difference to her.

"Get acquainted," I said to John in an incredibly patronizing tone, and then ran off before he could say another word.

My plan was to leave them alone for two hours. I went back to my apartment, retrieved a shopping list, and went to the supermarket.

I lolled down the aisles. Now that John Cerise was on Clara's case I had a tremendous feeling of confidence that everything would be all right. In fact, I was so confident I bought a Sara Lee chocolate cake to serve John when I got back.

When I finished my shopping list I took a slow walk around the neighborhood, luxuriating in the suddenly pleasant weather.

Then I headed home, pulling my shopping cart lightly.

When I turned the corner of my block and could see the stoop of my building, I knew something was wrong.

Police cars and an ambulance choked the street. A crowd had gathered.

As I reached the building, pushing my way through the onlookers, I saw the stretcher coming down the steps.

A leg with a white linen covering stuck out from beneath the EMS sheet.

"John," I screamed, letting go of my shopping cart and rushing to the stretcher.

It was him. His face looked like hamburger meat streaked with red dye number nine. There was blood splattered all over his body and clothes.

He smiled at me weakly. He reached up and patted my hand.

"Who are you, lady?" a burly man in an open blue shirt asked.

"I live up there," I replied. "What happened?" My composure had returned but I really couldn't comprehend what I was seeing.

Then I saw the badge hanging around his neck like a charm.

"Someone broke in. Your friend on the stretcher got in the way. But he'll be all right. He looks worse than he is. The thief got away."

"What about Clara?"

"He was alone."

"No, Clara is a cat. A white cat." I held my

hands out to show him the size; to show him that Clara was a small animal.

"There was no cat in the apartment, lady. Listen, you don't look so good. Why don't you sit down on the steps for a minute? Your friend is going to be all right."

I sat down and watched them load poor John into the ambulance.

6

John Cerise grinned when he saw me at the door of the hospital room. Once again he was dressed in white. The left side of his face was discolored and there was a bandage over his left eye. He looked smaller in bed, much, much smaller, like a kitten in a high chair. He made a motion with his hand and I approached.

"Did you find the cat?" he whispered. The discoloration was like a brilliantly painted bruise—red and black and purple.

I shook my head. The cat had vanished. The detective had surmised that the cat had run out of the apartment, down the steps, and onto the street.

An old man in evident pain lay on the other bed in the room. He made a valiant effort to wave at me. I patted him gently on the arm as I made my way between the beds. What else could I do?

"I'm sorry I got you into this mess," I said to John.

He shook his head with as much vigor as he could summon, to assure me he bore me no grudge. Then he seemed to gulp air. He finally said: "Alice, Clara is not an Abyssinian. But she is a lovely cat. She looks like an Abyssinian. She walks like an Abyssinian. She talks like an Abyssinian. . . ." He sat up with some effort, raising his hand for emphasis. "But there is no such thing as a white Abyssinian."

I pushed his arm down to his side and helped him back down.

"The police told me," I said, "that a thief must have known Mrs. Oshrin went away, and then broke in, not knowing anyone was there. It was just one of those odd coincidences; you being in the wrong place at the wrong time."

He nodded. He twisted in the bed. He started to get up again, thought the better of it, and said pathetically: "I never saw who it was, Alice. I was in the living room. Clara was on the rug. We were getting to know each other. I heard a noise. It sounded like someone was fumbling around near the door. But I thought it was you. I didn't even turn around. And then I felt a terrible pain here. . . ." He gestured to the side of his face. "And then everything went black."

"You were hit with one of Mrs. Oshrin's antique candle holders," I told him.

He closed his eyes.

"It could have been worse," I quipped, "you could have been hit with Mrs. Oshrin."

He grinned, his eyes still closed. The sun was streaming into the room.

"I'll be out of here tomorrow," he said.

"Do you want me to come here tomorrow to help you check out?" I asked.

"No need. I'll be fine."

I walked around his bed and sat down on the chair by the window. Cerise seemed to doze. A painkiller, I thought.

It was bizarre how things got out of hand. A stupid young man falls in love with a teacher. He gives her a cat. The teacher places the cat with a neighbor. The neighbor is unhappy. The teacher calls a friend to look the cat over. A thief breaks in and almost murders the friend, who has absolutely nothing to do with anyone or anything in that apartment.

The absurd chain of events horrified me. But something else about the whole mess was just plain peculiar. The detective had said that the thief panicked when he saw Cerise, hit him, and fled. That's why nothing had been taken from the apartment.

I had the nagging doubt, suspicion, feeling—call it what you will—that the thief had broken in to steal Clara; that is what I felt. But the logic escaped me.

Sitting on the hospital chair, thinking those thoughts, I did feel stupid. Clara was a lovely cat, but why would anyone break into an apartment to steal her? No, the detective was right: it was simply an aborted breaking and entering, aborted by an unexpected guest in the apartment. So then why did I have that feeling? Oh, glorious, delicious, irrelevant paranoia. Alice Nestleton, the quirky out-of-work actress, the New School lecturer, the well-known cat-sitter, the obscure crime solver—getting delusional once again over a rather dim-witted feline.

Cerise was talking to me. I had been so lost in my thoughts that I hadn't heard a word he said. Then I realized he was asking me where I really got the cat. He had known all the time I wasn't telling him the unvarnished truth.

"From a lovesick student," I admitted.

"Still breaking hearts?" he asked.

"The young man isn't old enough to be my nephew. I'm teaching a class at the New School. And there he was, an obnoxious young man of about twenty-odd years with a very bad case of arrested adolescence."

"You didn't want the cat?"

"John," I explained, "he dumped it on my landing in a box—his conception of a love offering, I suppose. I didn't even know it was a cat. I thought it was just a large box with a muffler or something like that inside, or maybe an extended love poem."

"Cat in a box," he mused, and then winced. Too much talking obviously hurt the side of his face.

"John," I said, "stop talking. Anyway, what is there to talk about? I don't even know if it was his cat. Maybe he found it on the street."

"Poor Clara," he whispered.

I leaned back in my chair. The next class at the New School was in forty-eight hours. If that young fool Bruce Whateverhisnameis didn't show up, I was determined to find out his last name even if I had to pester the New School's administrative staff. He had already caused the pain of a dear friend, the alienation of a treasured neighbor, and the disappearance or even worse of a lovely white cat with black spots on face and rump. His only redeeming trait seemed to be that he had taken the time to pay his last respects to a pathetic New York theatrical legend named Arkavy Reynolds.

7

The lovesick troublemaker, again, didn't show up in class. I waited twenty minutes, then told the class to keep itself busy, and walked resolutely to the administrative office. Only a clerk was at the desk, usual in the evenings.

I asked to see my class roster. She refused. I demanded. She waffled. I cajoled. She averted her eyes. I begged, hinting that I was only asking because of a health emergency. She didn't ask me to elaborate. That was sufficient. She showed it to me.

His name was Bruce Chessler. He lived at an address on East Fifth Street between First Avenue and Avenue A.

Then, armed with this information, I went back to the class and gave one of the most boring and irrelevant lectures in the entire history of adult education. At the end of the class I felt ashamed of myself, cursing Bruce Chessler again because it was his fault . . . everything was becoming his fault.

I went home and conversed with my cats. Bushy seemed quite understanding, even favoring me with four or five paw swipes.

There was no Bruce Chessler listed in the

Manhattan phone book at that address. I called information. There was no phone of any kind listed to any individual with that name.

Was I being obsessive? The thought occurred to me. Why didn't I just leave it alone? The cat was gone, God knows where. John Cerise would be okay. Mrs. Oshrin would forgive me. Yes, indeed—why didn't I leave it alone!

I began to pace. Then I walked to the hall mirror and stared at myself. Still thin, still lovely, still more golden than gray. Was that it? A middle-aged woman really fascinated by a young man who had fallen in love with her. No, I wasn't that stupid.

My antennae told me a crime had been committed. What was the crime? Simple. Someone had stolen Clara. That was what I believed from the first moment the detective had recounted his version of the events. There was no real proof . . . there was no real evidence.

But the logic of my belief was becoming more and more apparent as I thought about it.

Mrs. Oshrin had left on the trip very suddenly.

If her apartment had been targeted, she would have had to be under twenty-four-hour surveillance.

Why would someone be waiting for her to leave? She had absolutely nothing of value in her apartment.

It didn't make sense.

No, it was either a random break-in or a theft of the cat. One or the other. If it was a random break-in, any one of seven hundred individuals in my neighborhood could have been guilty. If it was a cat theft—who? The young man stealing his cat back? Absurd. A ring of cat thieves? But how would they know a cat was living with Mrs. Oshrin? In fact, had just arrived in her apartment. And why would they want Clara?

The whole thing was very strange, very perplexing, very engaging.

There was no doubt about it. I was going to pay a visit to young lovesick Bruce Chessler and find out all about vanished Clara. But I didn't want to go there by myself. I wanted company.

The next morning I called Anthony Basillio at his place of business—the Mother Courage Copying Shop.

Basillio was an old acting-school friend of mine who had long ago given up the theater in his head—but not in his heart. He had helped me out in the Long Island murders, and even though he sometimes got carried away . . . even though he still called me Swede . . . even though he still propositioned me ever so subtly . . . even though he still looked like a long-lost refugee from a long-haired ashram—I trusted him very much and I appreciated his kind of manic intelligence. To him, two and two were rarely four—but they were rarely five either. More important, he had that intense free-floating anxiety that made him long to do something, anything, which is, I suppose, why he gambled too much and probably did a lot of other things too much.

We agreed to meet at a coffee shop on East Eighth Street just before noon.

I got there about eleven-thirty. He was waiting and very happy to see me again, blowing into his hands as if he was about to embark on something extremely pleasurable—almost juicy. He looked exactly the same. His hair was getting longer. His face was breaking out again. How could a forty-year-old man continue to look so unfinished? Actually, I found it charming.

"Swede, Swede, Swede," he said as we sipped our Mexican coffee. I had long since given up any hope of him discarding that traditional nickname. No matter how many times I told him I was not of Swedish descent, he never believed me. But then again, all people who come from Minnesota originally, Basillio probably calls Swede.

"I have been longing, Swede, to hook up with you again. You're the only lady who brings me back."

"Back where, Tony?"

"Who the hell knows?"

We laughed.

"Who do you have to find?"

"A young man who was in my class at the New School. It's a long story," I replied.

"Tell it to me."

I told him.

"Are you afraid of this character?" he asked. I didn't answer for a while. He had a point. Why, in fact, was I afraid to find him alone? I knew the neighborhood. He hadn't been violent—only crazy.

"I'm very nervous around young men who are passionately in love with me," I replied. But that really wasn't the reason. I simply couldn't articulate the threat.

"Then you should be afraid of me, Swede."

"A married man with children?" I replied.

He grinned and changed the subject. "What's new with you? Any parts? Anything happening in the great beast?"

"I'm reading a crazy script—about a family of rats."

"Why not?" He laughed.

We finished our coffee and left. Five minutes later we stood in front of Chessler's four-story tenement building. It was like a hundred thousand others on the Lower East Side.

The day had become very hot and very muggy. It was the kind of August day in New York when you want to think only about distant galaxies. Nothing will ease your torment other than the vision of enormous explosions and implosions on a cosmic scale.

The building had two step-down stores on either side of the entrance. One was boarded up. The other was a shoemaker.

"Do you remember that fat woman who used to live down here?" Basillio asked. "The one who was in the Dramatic Workshop with us. I think it was in seventy-four. She was from North Carolina. She used to give parties. I think it was on Fourth Street."

I didn't remember. That was a long time ago. And if I did remember, it would probably be very depressing. There is nothing as sad as doomed theatrical careers. They are so predictable.

We walked into the small lobby. There was a panel of bells but the names next to them were so faded or mutilated that they couldn't be made out. No matter how intensely I stared at all those letters, not one of them seemed to combine into "Chessler."

"We can wait until someone comes down and ask," Basillio said.

Suddenly the outer door opened and a Hispanic woman with an enormous bizarre wig moved inside the small lobby with us.

"Who you? What you want?" she demanded. Her tone was very aggressive. She was carrying a large pail with sponges floating around on top.

"I'm looking for Bruce Chessler's apartment," I said.

She crossed herself.

"All his stuff now in cellar. I couldn't wait longer. No longer. Very sorry. It all downstairs. Owner told me to put it there. I put it there."

"But where is he?" I asked, confused by her comments.

She crossed herself again.

"I thought you his family. Young man dead. Murdered in bar on Eighth Street. Few days ago. You not his family?"

"Murdered?" My chest felt like a bellows.

"Boom! Boom!" she said. "Shot in head. Dead."

I leaned against the wall, suddenly dizzy. Basillio pulled me away because my shoulders were pushing five bells at once.

8

Next to Chessler's building was a building with an orange stoop and on that stoop Basillio and I sat for a very long time in the humid air. The breeze was fetid.

I had gotten over the initial shock. After all, I hardly knew the young man. I could barely remember his face. But there was a lingering disturbance . . . a kind of blanket over the head, very light, very well-knit, very hard to shake. What had he said to me in the funeral parlor? Something from Ben Jonson: "Beneath this rock there doth lie all the beauty that could ever die." Or was it "stone" rather than "rock"?

"We should look over his stuff," Basillio said.

"Why? We didn't even know him." The bitterness in my own voice astonished me.

"Because," Basillio explained, "if he's been dead a few days and nobody came for his stuff, it may mean his family doesn't know . . . that the cops couldn't locate next-of-kin. So we should look through his stuff, find out who he is . . . I mean who he was . . . and contact his people."

Basillio was absolutely right. It was the

proper thing to do. But I wasn't able to move. It was suddenly nice sitting there. There was all kinds of activity on the street to take my mind elsewhere. It was, in fact, what I had come to New York for, originally, from Minnesota, many years ago—for action, for all kinds of action if I may use that very ugly but very descriptive word: action in life, action in love, action in theater.

I was wearing one of my long country dresses, the kind that accentuates my already excessive height, the kind that my ex-husband used to say made me look like an erotic fantasy out of Virginia Woolf. I realized that I fitted quite well in the East Village.

"There she is," Basillio said.

The woman with the wig was standing in front of the house staring at the door as if deciding whether or not it had to be cleaned.

We got up. We walked toward her. She knew what we were doing. She pulled a large key ring from her pocket, shook the keys at us, and we followed her through the door into the lobby, through the hallway, and down a very steep staircase that led to a cellar filled with more junk than I had ever seen in my life.

We heard scurrying among the objects. Cats? Rats? Derelicts? Junkies? Ghosts?

"Pigeons," said the woman leading us, with a broad grin. I couldn't tell whether she was being sarcastic or truthful. I realized also that she was not Hispanic, that the accent was something like Lebanese.

We walked through another door to a less-cluttered and better-lit space which had obviously once been the coal room and still had the partitions. She led us to one partition, piled with cartons and clothes and posters and toasters. She crossed herself and held out a hand in explanation—that this was what was left of Bruce Chessler. Then she was gone.

Anthony Basillio shook his head slowly as he stared at the stuff.

"We should, I suppose, be looking for something that identifies his family," he said.

I nodded. It seemed the intelligent way to proceed. A single overhead uncovered bulb burned ferociously down on the remains.

We started on the first large carton—Tony on one side and me on the other, emptying the contents carefully, almost religiously. About thirty seconds into the emptying, I was overwhelmed with such a sense of sadness, of futility, of hatred of whatever had extirpated him, that I just sat down on a low carton and started to cry. Above all, I couldn't deal with the memory of what the landlady or janitress had said. She had said: "Boom! Boom!" The young man had been shot to death. It was like an earthquake had been telescoped into one inconceivable splatter of violence. Steel. Noise. Blood. Pulp.

Basillio kept on, happily leaving me alone. I had the absurd notion, sitting there as I wept, that Clara, the white cat Bruce had given me to express his infatuation with an older woman—wherever Clara was now, she knew and was weeping also, as cats weep, from the stomach.

I could see Basillio removing book after book and flipping pages—waiting for that telltale postcard or check stub used as a page marker which would identify him further. Then the magazines and the records and the pieces of a life on paper—menus, clippings, God knows what.

I wanted to help but I couldn't. Now I was beginning to see his face . . . and that sport shirt . . . and hear his caustic classroom mode . . . but now it was not threatening . . . death had given him a certain élan in my mind . . . the tragedy was becoming personally more intense, more intimate.

There were clothes and hats and beat-up sneakers. There were old check stubs and some canceled checks from the Chemical Bank branch on Eighth Street and Broadway.

Then Basillio pulled out a very fat white envelope, sealed with a thick ugly rubber band. He pulled the rubber band off, opened the envelope, and peered inside.

"Here," he said, bringing it over to me, "this is very sad."

Indeed it was. There were dozens of photographs in the envelope. Some of Bruce Chessler. Some of unidentified people. Some of Bruce in a group. It was his photo album of sorts.

In some of them he posed, wearing that chip-on-the-shoulder smile . . . the kind that said: I'm smarter and tougher and hipper than you and you'd better know it. Some of them showed a more pensive side, particularly when he was photographed with someone else. And sometimes, in the younger photos, he looked just plain desperate.

I came to the photo of an old woman.

I stared at it—the woman wore braids wrapped around her head. She wore a high-necked, very old-fashioned dress with a large ornament around her neck on a thick chain.

I moved on. Then suddenly I shuffled back to the old woman. The woman was old, but the photo was not. Maybe five years old at the most—the sides were still white and crisp.

The more I looked at the photo, the more I realized that I knew the old woman.

The hair, the ornament, the dress—they were all familiar.

Then I remembered.

"Tony," I said, "come here for a minute."

He came back over. I showed him the photo.

"Do you know who this is?" I asked.

"No."

"Look hard!"

"I'm looking. But I don't know."

"Does the name Maria Swoboda mean anything to you?"

He cocked his head and screwed up his face. He was going through his thinking contortions.

Then he snapped his fingers: "The old acting teacher."

"Right," I confirmed, "the Method-acting teacher from the Moscow Art Theater. She had a studio in New York in the fifties, sixties, and early seventies—on Grove Street. For a time she was the rage. I remember when I first came to New York I was able to get a few lessons from her, and I considered myself in the presence of a high priestess.''

Yes, I remembered that crazy, wonderful old lady very well. But Method acting had long since gone out of vogue and I had no idea whether she was still alive, much less still teaching. She had not been a young woman when I went to her.

"Was Chessler an actor?" Basillio asked.

"Well, he was taking my class; he obviously had some interest in the theater. But he didn't talk like an actor. He talked like a political radical. You know . . . a lot of passion . . . a lot of hate . . . a lot of Brecht—like you used to talk, Tony. And he did show up at Arkavy Reynolds' funeral. You knew he died, didn't you? He got into a fight with a homeless man who murdered him on Jane Street. Two fools. Do you remember that fat man?''

Basillio nodded and went back to his work. I kept staring at the picture. God, how the memories surfaced . . . of Madame Swoboda, which was what she was called . . . speaking about Stanislavski and the vision they all had . . . speaking about the character being inside of the actor . . . speaking of how the character can only emerge authentically if the actor utilizes his own creativity, his own beauty, his own suffering to project the character from within to without. It was heady stuff. It was glorious.

Basillio interrupted my memories. He handed me a sheaf of papers that had been rolled and fastened with another rubber band.

"This is even sadder," he said.

I held the top and bottom of one sheet so it wouldn't fold. It was a handwritten letter.

It was to me.

Dear Alice Nestleton:

   You think I'm an idiot, don't you? You think I torment you in class to cause you grief. Don't you realize I must differentiate myself from all the others in any and every way possible? Don't you understand that I am the only one in this stupid class who knows you are a great actress? I love you very much and I am afraid to tell you. I have a fantasy about you . . . a sexual fantasy . . . all the time . . . we are in a house built of reeds . . . it is high above some body of blue water . . . the house is on stilts and we are making love and you are wearing a beautiful . . .

I didn't want to read any further. I crumpled the sheaf of papers and thrust it into my bag. Basillio was right. Was there anything sadder than love letters not sent by a dead boy?

9

It was like a scene from an Edwardian melodrama. I sat on the edge of the bed. The love letters were scattered over the sheet in disarray. I was literally unable to read them except for very tiny snatches. It was too painful. He obviously hadn't known me at all. He was fantasizing. The saddest parts of all were his erotic fantasies, which he described in painful detail. There were twenty-two letters in all.

The first one was obviously written immediately after he attended the first class in the New School. He described what I wore and what I said during that first class. Bruce Chessler was older than I had thought—about twenty-five. And it was obvious to me now that his bizarre behavior in class was a function of his condition. He was unable to make contact with the object of his deranged love—myself—so he could only attack me. He understood that he was causing me distress, and his letters were full of apologies.

I wanted to read them thoroughly and carefully but I couldn't.

Basillio called me about twenty minutes before midnight. He told me that he had checked out Swoboda, my old teacher, whose picture was inexplicably in Bruce Chessler's belongings. She had died four years ago in Lakewood, New Jersey. When he hung up I gathered the love letters in a fury of frustration and literally stuffed them into one of my chests. The young man was dead. He had no family or friends. His cat, given to me out of disjointed love, was gone. At least John Cerise was fine.

I couldn't fall asleep until two, and when I did fall asleep I had a whole series of dreams about my first boyfriend in Minnesota and necking in one of the dairy barns while my grandmother was twenty feet away behind the partition and didn't know a thing was going on.

The first thing I thought of when I woke up was retrieving the love letters and reading them carefully. I fought back the impulse. It obviously had something to do with the dream.

I spent a great deal of the next hour staring out of my living-room window onto the street, hoping for a glimpse of Clara. Perhaps she had just run out onto the street and was living from garbage can to garbage can. Perhaps she was now living feral in one of the overgrown backyards that run like a scar between the two rows of houses that front the street—and can be reached and seen only through the basement apartments or the interior hallways on the ground floors or by fire escapes from the roofs. Why not? Maybe she was there. But I saw no beast that resembled the strange white cat Chessler had delivered to me.

When I finally pulled myself away from my obsessive nonsense of staring out the window to find Clara, I slipped into a very agitated depression. I started to pace back and forth across the living room, stepping over Bushy each time. I was pacing so quickly in my agitation that Pancho even aborted one of his rushes to stare at me reflectively. Maybe he was thinking: Ah, the fool now knows what I go through twenty-four hours a day. She finally realizes they are after her as well.

In fact, the last time I was feeling so bad in the head was when I started that *Romeo and Juliet* rehearsal in Montreal and I was frightened that the director, Portobello, would nip my interpretation of the Nurse in the bud.

I ceased my pacing when it dawned on me that if no one of Bruce Chessler's family had been found to claim his belongings or identify his body—it was the landlady who had done that—then there had to be no one to claim the body. And that meant that the young man, sport shirt and all, had been buried in one of those horrible derelict graves on small islands in the East River. I had once read about them—about how convicts from Rikers Island dig the graves, and the anonymous bodies, mostly from the Bowery and its environs, are slipped into them . . . like omelets.

I found that unbearable. But it was too late. The young man was already interred.

Things in my head were starting to get out of hand. I remembered part of one of the young man's fantasies—a house made of reeds. For the first time the imagery seemed familiar. From Yeats? I couldn't recall. From Euripides?

"Boom! Boom!" the landlady had said. Shot in a bar.

Why did Bruce Chessler die? That was the stupid question that aborted it all—that aborted my agitated depression; it was like a Zen koan, focusing all my energies. Why was it important to know? Because he loved me? Because I didn't reciprocate? Was it guilt? Old-fashioned corrosive guilt?

Why did Bruce Chessler die? Forget the white cat. Forget the beating of John Cerise. Forget the photo of my old drama teacher. Forget the love letters. Forget the funeral of Arkavy Reynolds. Forget Bruce's obnoxious behavior in my class. Forget everything.

Why had he died? Boom! Boom! Why?

No one asked me to inquire. No one paid me to inquire. There was no quid pro quo.

I just picked up the phone and called various numbers within the New York Police Department as listed in the telephone book. I was switched to an information officer and then to an assistant to a precinct commander and then to the civilian review board and then to a divisional spokesperson (whatever that meant), until finally, hours later, numb and dumb, I found myself talking to a detective named Harold Hanks. He was in a hurry.

He asked me if I was a relative of Bruce Chessler's.

I said no.

Then he asked me if I had any information concerning the murder.

I said no.

Now he really was in a hurry to get rid of me. I went into one of my acting modes: a woman who has lost a "son" . . . a "child" . . . a student . . . a brilliant young mind cut off, etc., etc.

To get me off the phone he said that he had to be at the Gramercy Park Hotel at about two—and I should meet him on the corner, where Lexington ends at the park, right across from the hotel.

So that's how I met Harry Hanks, a thin, nervous black man. He was waiting there for me when I arrived, with a scowl on his face as if I were late—which I wasn't.

"So Bruce Chessler was a student of yours?" he asked.

"Yes."

"And he was a brilliant student . . . a kid with a real academic career ahead of him . . . isn't that what you said on the phone?"

"Yes."

"Don't lie to me, lady, I'm tired. Okay. Here's what I know. What *we* know. The kid was a small-time 'speed' merchant—pills mostly, all kinds of meth and dex. He was shot to death in some kind of drug-related dispute. The kid was sitting at a back table in a bar called Halliday's on Eighth and First. About three in the morning a character with a beard, about fifty, walks in and sits down next to him. He and Chessler talk. Then they argue. The guy shoots the kid in the head and walks out. The weapon used was a twenty-five-caliber semiautomatic pistol. We found four hundred 'greens' on the kid and six hundred dollars in cash."

A twenty-five-caliber semiautomatic pistol? My forehead broke into a cool sweat.

He opened a stick of gum, folded it, and placed it into his mouth, signaling that he was finished with his information briefing; that it was all he knew and he really wasn't exercised over the whole matter.

Then he grinned and said: "Oh, yeah, I forgot. The kid was also an out-of-work actor."

"Yes, I'm aware of that." My voice was abstract.

"Well, what else do we got to say to each other?"

"Was the weapon a Beretta?" I asked quietly.

"Yes. How did you know?"

"I guessed." His mention of a twenty-five-caliber semiautomatic handgun had jolted me into a connection. It was suddenly very odd to me that Arkavy Reynolds and Bruce Chessler had both been murdered by the same kind of weapon. And one had showed up at the other's funeral.

"These kinds of cases," Hanks said in a patronizing way, "get solved eight years later by mistake, or they don't get solved at all. Speed kills, lady, like the man says." He walked away. It was very hot. I looked across the street into the posh park through the railings. Two white-coated nannies were pushing carriages, around and around and around. Why did Bruce Chessler die?

10

It took me six hours to locate and meet with Detective Felix of Manhattan South Homicide. He was one of the two police officers who had visited me in the New School after class and asked me to identify photographs of people who attended Arkavy Reynolds' wake on Madison Avenue. Felix agreed to come to my apartment only after I told him I had important evidence concerning Arkavy's murder.

He seemed nervous when he entered my apartment, staring at Bushy with a hint of fear in his eyes. "He doesn't bite or scratch," I said. Detective Felix was wearing a spanking-clean button-down blue shirt and a lovely soft gray suit. How different he was from Detective Hanks! He made a few inquiries about the current state of my theatrical career and then sat down gingerly on my sofa, very gingerly, as if the cats could give him some sort of communicable disease.

Once he had seated himself and demurely opened the buttons of his jacket, he asked: "Do you remember a play about Joan of Arc starring Julie Harris?"

"I do," I replied, "but I forget the name of

the play. Anyway, I think it was before your time. Did you see it?"

"No," he admitted. Then there was an awkward silence. He was looking at me very intently.

"Well, what do you have for me?" he finally asked.

Have? Did he want coffee? Chocolate milk? A beer? Then I remembered that it was simply a police expression.

"That young man, that student of mine, who went to the funeral home for Arkavy's wake . . . he was murdered by a twenty-five-caliber semiautomatic Beretta a short time later. The same kind that killed your informer."

Felix guffawed. "It's a very common street weapon now. These things go in cycles. One year the fad is twenty-two-caliber Longs . . . the next year all the bad guys are using .357 Magnums. This year it's twenty-five-caliber Berettas. So what?"

"Did you do a ballistic check on the bullets?" I asked, trying to sound knowledgeable but not accusatory.

"No! Why should we have done that? There was no connection at the time. The murders were in different places and different jurisdictions. And it can't be done now. It would require too much paperwork and too many goddamn signatures without enough jurisdiction."

I finally sat down at the other end of the sofa. Detective Felix looked even more uncomfortable now. He ran one hand through his brilliantly cut short haircut. One could still see the scissor marks.

"You told me at the New School that Arkavy had become a police informant. I suppose you mean that he had been arrested on some charge and you let the charges drop in exchange for his continuing cooperation."

"Right."

"What was his crime?"

"Possession of amphetamines with intent to sell."

I exhaled. "Well," I noted, "that young man, Bruce Chessler, was an amphetamine pusher. When he was murdered he had a few hundred pills on him."

"Do you mean the fat man and this student of yours were business associates?"

"Why else would he go to the funeral?"

Detective Felix grinned wickedly at me, as if I were some kind of bumbling idiot, and then said: "You mean there was speed stashed in the coffin? Or do you mean pushers like to pay their last respects because they're so filled with compassion?"

I did feel like an idiot. Because I believed Bruce Chessler had gone to the funeral home for some nostalgic tribute to a lost tradition personified by the fat man. But the speed connection had seemed to me to be the right one for the detective—the one he would find logical, palatable. Wrong again.

"Besides," Felix continued, showing a trace of alarm as big bad Bushy began to walk stiff-legged around the sofa, "Arkavy hadn't touched or dealt that stuff for two years."

"Are you sure?"

"Of course I'm sure," he said contemptuously, "because I even tried to give him some stuff to keep him happy, but he said he was getting his kicks from other things now."

"What things?"

"Maybe boys," he said, "or maybe older actresses."

I flushed. His comment infuriated me, but it may have been unintentional. He was beginning to act a little like Bruce Chessler. I hoped he wasn't getting amorous.

I left the sofa and sat at the large dining-room table, along the wall, leafing through some papers.

"Well," I finally said, "I'm sorry to have wasted your time."

He stood up quickly. "Look . . . thanks for the information. If you hear anything else, let me or my partner know. Maybe they did know each other in the past. Maybe they did business together when the fat man was into speed. Why not? But as for the twenty-five Beretta . . . it's meaningless. There are thousands of them on the street. If you're going to get blown away—why not with one of those? And pushers and crazies always get blown away sooner or later."

"But I thought you told me you wanted very much to get his killer."

"We do."

"Well, if there's a good chance that the same man who murdered Reynolds murdered Chessler . . . or even a slim chance . . . shouldn't you start looking into Chessler's murder? I know the detective working on his case. His name is—"

Felix held up his hand, stopping me. "We'll get the one who killed the fat man. Believe me."

He carefully buttoned his suit jacket, signaling me that the interview was over. I let him out and heard him skip down the stairs as if he had been released from a mental ward.

The meeting with him had exhausted me. Once again I had discovered—a lesson I seemed to have to learn again and again— that police departments cannot handle obscurity. They flee from it. They need defined objects. They flee from obscure people and obscure deaths and obscure connections. Like a cat approaching a rosebush. It was I, not the NYPD, who was going to have to unravel these obscurities.

11

"Listen, Swede, you're not acting rationally. This is not a rational decision," Basillio said, nudging Bushy's tail with his foot. Bushy ignored him. Pancho was staring at the stranger from beneath the long table, crouched, ready to flee.

I had called Basillio and asked him to come over even though it was a long drive from Fort Lee and his wife might go crazy. I had told him what I planned to do . . . to pursue the question: Why did the young man die? I told him that I wanted to start hanging out for a while at the bar in which Bruce Chessler was murdered. I had told him that I needed his help. I needed him to accompany me—to provide, as you will, the cover.

"Swede, listen. This isn't like those murders out on Long Island. The cops there were baffled, and every conclusion they came to was stupid. You had to intercede. It was a question of . . ." He hesitated, searching for a word, then said: ". . . justice. If you hadn't gotten involved, they would never have caught the murderers. Because the whole thing was bizarre and out of the cops' comprehension. But here we have a pill-pushing kid murdered. This, the cops deal with every day. They aren't obligated to understand what you're talking about."

"Do you want to help me or not?" I persisted.

"This kid, this Chessler. I don't care if he was in love with you. I don't care if he was an out-of-work actor who had a picture of your old acting teacher. He was a druggie, Swede, a hustler. There's no confusion. There's no puzzle. It was a goddamn drug deal gone wrong. The kid had hundreds of pills and plenty of bucks in his pocket. He was a dealer. You *know* why he died and how he died. Like the cop told you, it's that old slogan: speed kills. God, I haven't heard that slogan in years."

He was getting agitated, almost yelling at me.

"Calm down, Tony."

"Okay. I'm calm. Can we talk about this? Do you really think they snuffed him out because of a crazy white cat?"

"I don't know," I said, and I really didn't. The Arkavy Reynolds connection, real or imagined, had tempered a lot of my flights of fancy and intuition.

He started to walk about the apartment, shaking his head.

"Tony, do you remember Theresa Lombardo?"

"No. Should I?"

"Think back. Remember the Dramatic Workshop. Remember her?"

He stopped and stared at me. "That small dark girl. A very good actress. Right?"

"Right. You remember her."

"So what?"

"Remember how crazy she was about being an actress . . . about how nothing on earth—and I mean nothing—meant a god-damn thing to her except the theater."

"A lot of us thought like that then."

"Sure. But Theresa was a very poor girl. Do you remember how she supported herself?"

"No."

"She turned tricks."

"Oh, here we go . . . hearts and flowers. Are you telling me this kid sold speed because of his great love for the theater?"

"I don't know. I know nothing about him. Neither do the police. I'm just making a point."

"About what?"

"About theater people. About actors and actresses and directors. About their heads and hearts."

He sat down on the sofa. Our conversation had obviously exhausted him.

Then he said: "I'll make a point. Here I am, a forty-two-year-old failed theatrical designer who makes more money than he knows what to do with, simply by making Xerox copies of company reports—talking to a forty-one-year-old actress with enormous talent who is forced to cat-sit for a living because she can't stand either Broadway or Hollywood and all it represents and she's determined to blaze her own avant-garde path when she's not solving bizarre crimes. . . . Here we both are, discussing a young pill pusher who gets blown away. . . . Don't you see, Swede? The whole thing is crazy."

He leaned forward and stared at Bushy, who was sitting up like an oversize Egyptian cat, perhaps startled by Tony's rhetoric. Bushy didn't like excessive chatter. It interfered with his naps.

"I hope, Swede," he continued, "that when a disgruntled customer blows me away you'll start an investigation as to why I died. After all, I loved you also."

"But you never wrote me letters that you didn't send," I quipped.

"You should know," he said, and I suddenly felt very uncomfortable.

There was a long awkward silence. Basillio started to play with his car keys.

"Okay, Swede, I'll take the part."

"Thanks, Tony."

"But remember, my limit is two drinks. So if I'm sitting with you in that bar and you let me go over that limit and I start getting wild—it'll be on your lovely head."

He left without another word to me or to Bushy or to Pancho.

12

When one walked into Halliday's, one first saw a cigarette machine on the left. To the right was a small horseshoe bar with a mirror and a TV set behind it. The walls had innocuous beer emblems pasted or fastened on. An eclectic new jukebox was against the left wall. Walk through the partition, and there's a pay phone and the "dining area"—tables, two booths, pinballs, video games. But in fact, no food is served. And only three bottle beers. During the day it's a local bar—Ukrainians, lost souls, and passersby. Between seven and eight in the evening the younger set starts coming in—black leather, musicians, young shirt-and-ties on a night out, students, architects, urban planners, poets, and an assortment of bizarre persons at the many fringes of the art world.

The bartenders are old East European men—all short. No waiters or waitresses. You buy your drink at the bar and take it to the tables if you wish, or just stand around and drink. Two bouncers are visible: one, an enormous, silent, lazy Slav; and a thin one who doubles as a cleanup man and busboy. The front of the establishment is fairly well lit; the "dining area" is very dark.

It was seven-thirty on a Tuesday evening when Basillio and I walked in. We bought two mixed drinks at the bar—Bloody Marys—and went to one of the tables in the rear.

The place was beginning to fill. Basillio had constructed our cover theatrically: a married couple from New Jersey, dressed absurdly, seeking an authentic East Village milieu, desiring to see the denizens, to soak in what the East Village still promised—a heady whiff of undiluted bohemianism. Basillio wore a banker suit topped with an outlandish tie. I wore a lot of jewelry on a very flimsy, very sexy, and very gauche silk blouse and silk pants. I wore high heels, raising my normal tallness to Amazonian levels. It was all a bit much, but Basillio relished his new directorial and costume assignments.

"Jesus," Basillio whispered to me, "it looks like a set for *Lost Weekend,* designed by a guy who can only use crayons. I may have read the scene wrong."

An hour went by. The tables and booths filled. The bar was three deep. The noise went from a soft hum to a soft roar. We could hear snatches of conversation—about paintings, about plays, about sports, about the subways, about books, about who was in the bar and why.

"I don't want to be aggressive, Swede, but what the hell are we looking for?"

"Regulars," I said. "I want to identify regulars who might have known Bruce Chessler."

He nodded and grinned. "Remember that bar on the West Side we used to go to after class?"

"Very well," I replied. "That was in one of your earlier reincarnations, Tony, as a theatrical barfly."

We reminisced about the old times, about the cat he used to bring to class in a shopping bag, about our teachers, about old acquaintances whom we both had lost contact with. This undercover work was becoming enjoyable.

By the time ten o'clock rolled around we had identified three possibles: a young couple dressed all in black who sat in the adjoining booth and who had their hands clasped tightly across the table and were speaking low and passionately to each other; a slim, small black woman with a close-cropped head who sat doodling with a pencil in the near-darkness at one of the tables; and a very old man who had a breathing problem and carried a canvas bag with a New York Mets logo.

We left the bar at eleven-thirty and came back the next two nights.

On the third night I thanked Basillio and dispensed with his services because I knew that the black woman was the one I had to contact—she was there every night in the same spot with the same doodling pencil and with the same bottle of virtually untouched Rolling Rock beer in front of her.

Her name was Elizabeth and she smiled when I asked if I could join her. She gave her name freely, as if she were waiting and happy for some company.

A poet, she said she was. And what was I? An actress, I said. She nodded compassionately, as if I had tuberculosis or some other chronic disorder.

"I notice," I said, "that you never drink your beer."

"I don't drink alcohol."

I didn't know what to say except to ask her why she didn't, then, sit in a coffee shop rather than a bar, but I decided against saying anything.

"And I only eat one meal a day," she added, "because I consider myself a disciple of Pantajali, and the appetite is just another vehicle that must be discarded."

"Who is Pantajali?" I asked.

She smiled sadly at me, as if my ignorance was not really my fault, but a function of my age and height and bad taste in clothes. She was wearing a beautifully simple sheath with sunflowers.

"Pantajali was the founder of yogic philosophy."

"Ah," I replied, trying to sound properly apologetic.

"It was Pantajali who first understood that the source of the great cosmic tragedy was when consciousness became entwined with matter."

Elizabeth spoke very precisely, with a very odd accent—the origins of which I couldn't place. It was probably an affectation, because she was an obvious kook—but it was very charming and her voice was low and resonant and one wanted to hear her speak more.

However, it was time to get down to business.

"Were you here when that young man was shot to death a few days ago?"

"Of course," she said. "Of course I was here. Right here."

We were silent for a while.

"Did you know him?"

"We had talked."

"I want to find out more about him," I said.

"Why?"

I didn't lie to her. I told her the truth to the best of my knowledge. I told her that he had been a student of mine at the New School. He had fallen in love with me. I simply wanted to know *why* he had died.

"Why?" she asked with a lilting inflection. "He died because the karmic forces are totally disjointed. Can't you see it all around you?"

I ignored her philosophy.

"The police," I said, "told me he got into an argument with an older man and the older man shot him to death."

"That is what happened," she affirmed.

"And you were there?"

"Here," she corrected, "right here. And he was shot here, right where I'm pointing."

"What did you do?"

"Nothing."

"Then what happened?"

"They came. The police and the ambulances. But he was dead. He didn't even slump over. There was a hole in his forehead. He was dead."

She reached over and patted my hand as if I were a child.

"Did he have any friends? Did he always come in here alone?"

"He came in with a woman sometimes."

"Who?"

"Her name is Risa."

"Is she here now?"

"No. I haven't seen her for some time. She wasn't here when he was shot."

"Do you know her last name?"

"Macros have no last names."

I didn't understand what she meant.

"What is 'macro'?"

"She's macrobiotic. She eats at that restaurant all the time, near Second Avenue. Sarah's—the macrobiotic restaurant."

Then she started to tell me how foolish it was to persist in my inquiry; that even if the young man loved me, love itself was absurd. It had no content. It was egoless and ownerless. It was an echo, for it resulted only from cause and condition. It was like a fire that consumed itself.

"Can you tell me what she looks like?" I asked, interrupting her philosophical flight, which was accompanied by a frenetic doodling of her pencil.

"Risa is short and heavy and her hair is

red," Elizabeth said—then made a motion with her hand to show me it was cut in neopunk style, half of the head straight up.

I sat back. Now finally I had a name and a body and a lead. I had someone who knew him well. I wanted to rush out of the bar to the macrobiotic restaurant, but I knew it was too late . . . the restaurant was closed by then. Tomorrow would be time. And I didn't want to leave Elizabeth. She had endeared herself to me. There was something so fey about her, so ephemeral . . . like a cat circling a dish of strange-smelling food. And she might know even more.

"Did you ever see him with a strange-looking fat man? A man who wore coveralls and a shirt and tie and a cabdriver's hat?"

She looked up intensely, as if trying to recreate in her mind my description of Arkavy Reynolds.

"Black or white?" she suddenly asked.

"White," I replied.

"No." Then she laughed. "If he was black, he might well be one of my uncles." She giggled nervously and fell silent. We sat together, oddly at ease with each other.

"Oh, look there," she said suddenly, pointing toward the bar.

I followed her point, found nothing, turned back to her for information, but she was already thinking of something else.

Yes, like a cat approaching strange food. I stayed there another two hours or so, listening to her intermittent lectures on food and the cosmos and karma, in fits and starts, with large doses of silence between.

Then I thanked her profusely and went home. Risa was the next stop.

13

When I saw her through the window—I was standing on the street peering in—the first thought that came to me was the incongruity of Bruce Chessler having this young woman as a lover and falling in love with me.

She was indeed stout and very young and very punk and her hair was very red.

From the window I could not identify what was on her plate—it looked like kelp and brown rice and sprouts. She was eating slowly, reflectively, chewing thoroughly.

I like people on macrobiotic diets even though I haven't the foggiest idea what they're doing—spiritually or nutritionally. After all, if you're not what you eat, what are you? Of course, I didn't believe the whole thing for a minute. A producer once asked me if I was macrobiotic. When I said no, he replied that I had that extreme slimness which often is symptomatic of either anorexia or a macrobiotic diet. I told him it came from poverty. He didn't think that was funny. But what would he make of Risa—a chunky macrobiotic? It would knock his theory to hell.

Anyway, Sarah's was packed. I waited outside. It was a full forty-five minutes before the young woman finished chewing all her food properly. Then she came out.

I waited until she had turned west on Eighth Street and started walking resolutely before I caught up to her.

"Excuse me. Did you know Bruce Chessler?" I thought the direct approach would be the best.

She stopped suddenly, as if she had been hit with a blunt object. She turned and stared at me.

"No, I didn't know him. I slept with him but I didn't know him. Who the hell are you?"

"Alice Nestleton. His teacher from the New School."

"Oh," she said sardonically, "his great unrequited love."

"Can I talk to you a minute?"

"About what? What is there to talk about now? He's dead. He was murdered."

"Yes, I know that."

She started to walk again, faster. I caught up with her and kept pace, not saying anything. She was mumbling to herself.

Finally, as we walked past Cooper Union, she stopped and whirled toward me, and this time she was crying.

She said: "What do you really want? What can I tell you? He's dead. For no reason."

I took her arm and guided her close to the building line. She didn't resist. She fumbled for a cigarette from her purse. She lit it and inhaled mightily.

"Tell me about him, please. It was all so strange. He showed up one evening, told me he loved me, and left a white cat—"

Risa held up one hand suddenly, interrupting. "A white cat?" she asked, incredulous.

"And the next day it was stolen," I said.

She laughed like a lunatic and threw her cigarette away.

"Don't feel bad," she said, "he left me *two* white cats and both of them vanished from my apartment during a robbery."

"Two white cats?"

"Two white cats."

"Tell me about him, Risa," I said, and my voice was kindly because I suddenly felt an enormous white-cat camaraderie with her.

"What can I say? He was a lunatic . . . a lovable junkie lunatic speed-freak alcoholic who wanted to be a great actor. But he hated theater people . . . he had only contempt for them . . . for all of them . . . and especially for his grandmother and her friends."

"Did he ever mention a man to you named Arkavy Reynolds?"

"You mean that crazy one with the hat . . . the one who was shot to death? I met him once. Bruce used to sell him speed. And sometimes they got into arguments about plays and scenes and directors. And once they got into a rough argument about his grandmother."

So that was the connection. Speed. Bruce sold Arkavy drugs. It was logical. I figured that was the case. But Detective Felix had thought the connection unimportant. And this thing with the grandmother was bizarre.

"Who was his grandmother, Risa? And what did she have to do with all this? With the theater?"

"His grandmother was Maria Swoboda."

The astonishment on my face was quite noticeable.

"Then you know of her," Risa said. "Yes, Maria Swoboda, the old Russian lady from the Moscow Art Theater ... the one who knew Stanislavski. Bruce hated her. And her friends—Bukai, Chederov, Mallinova—I think those are their names. Sometimes when he got high he used to rant for hours about them. That they were fakes, hustlers, idiots ... on and on he went."

"Where did he get the white cats?"

"I never knew. He never told me. But then again, he never told me a lot of things. I knew he took speed and sold the stuff. I knew he had devils in his head."

She choked back some tears, then continued in a strange, sad, husky voice, "Do you know how sad the city is? There are thousands of Bruce Chesslers wandering around. They don't even recognize each other. I'm a songwriter. I once wrote a piece called 'Soft Dreams in Hell'. But no one would buy it because it was about them. Do you understand? All these sad people wandering from street to street and they can't even recognize their own truth."

She seemed to be drifting. I brought her back to reality.

"You know, Maria Swoboda used to be a teacher of mine—years ago. In fact, I found a picture of her in Bruce's belongings, but it never dawned on me they were related."

She straightened her back as if determined not to make any more personal revelations. "Yep, a real old-fashioned grandma. That is, until she died."

"You mean he still ranted against her after she was dead?"

"Well, when I met him she was already dead. He talked about her as if she were alive."

She started to walk again, turning north on Fourth Avenue. She said: "I have to go . . . I have to go to the post office."

I stayed with her. We were a strange couple walking. No doubt the passersby constructed their own scenario—mother and child. Mother unhappy with punk antics of daughter. Mother and daughter going to a physician. How many scenarios were there? None of them remotely correct.

"There's the post office," she said, and I could tell by the way she stood that she was determined I should be gone.

"Can I talk to you again sometime?" I asked.

"About Bruce?"

"Yes. And other things."

"Other things," she repeated bitterly, and then wrote her phone number down on my wrist with a Magic Marker—right on the flesh. I was so shocked I didn't even protest. It was a subtle form of revenge perhaps . . . for

Bruce falling in love with an older woman. I snatched the Magic Marker from her hand and wrote my number on her wrist.

She ran into the post office. I started to walk home, trying somehow to cover the script on my flesh but not wanting it to be blurred until I could transcribe it.

As I walked I found myself enjoying the gathering heat. The young man had turned out to be much more perplexing dead than alive.

And the idea that now I knew of three white cats taken—three white cats placed by Bruce Chessler in inappropriate "foster" homes from which they were abducted—all that made me kind of inebriated with the absurdity of it. I realized, to my chagrin, that I had forgotten to ask the young girl whether her two white cats had the same black spots on face and rump as Clara—poor Clara.

As for Grandma Maria Swoboda—that was very difficult to believe. That they were related. Or was it more difficult to believe that he would hate his grandma? How could anyone hate Madame Maria Swoboda? Alive or dead? And why was it difficult to believe? Did I expect a twenty-five-year-old man living on the Lower East Side, who had been born in this country and never spoken anything other than English, to behave like a Russian theatrical personage? Did I bear any cultural resemblance to my dairy-farmer grandmother? I realized in fact that I did have such a resemblance. I walked like her. I looked like her. I was still a farmgirl at heart—well-read but unable to be sophisticated; cynical but unable to act in that mode; passionate but forced by circumstance into a kind of suspended celibacy.

It was odd how Bruce Chessler's strange relationship with his grandmother had started me thinking about mine. I rarely thought about her, for some reason, in hot weather. And when I did think about her, there was always one image that came to mind: whenever my grandmother had entered the dairy barn to check on the cows, she would, somehow, without saying a word, set all the barn cats into motion. As she walked down the sheds the cats would leap about—overhead, below, from side to side—as if my grandmother had choreographed them into a complex dance through some psychic power. And the moment my grandmother left the barn, they would cease.

I reached Twenty-third Street. The bank on the corner said it was ninety-one degrees at two-twenty-one in the afternoon.

I was getting weary. Only a few blocks more. It had been a long few days—bars, health-food restaurants, macrobiotics, Yoga, black woman poet, punk girl songwriter— yes, it had been exhausting.

And what I had found out about Bruce Chessler really didn't give me any good clue to the philosophical problem: Why did he die? Nor did anything I had learned really contradict the police story that he was shot to death in a drug-related incident.

What I had found was a completely new

and related crime—the kidnapping of three white cats who had been delivered to Risa and me by Bruce Chessler. What was going on?

14

Basillio laughed so hard that he almost fell off his swivel chair.

"You mean all our undercover work has revealed the astonishing fact that three goddamn white cats are missing?"

We were in his office in the back of the copying store. We could hear the copying machines whirring. We could see the customers clutching their papers.

I let him laugh. Until that very morning I had thought it funny also, from time to time. Well, not really funny, but like something from Mother Goose. But then I had begun to think carefully . . . to think about Bruce Chessler.

"No, we found out a bit more," I said.

"What?" he retorted. "That he hated his grandmother and in fact all Russian émigrés from the Moscow Art Theater? That the kid had an arrested adolescence? That he was another pathetic out-of-work actor living on egotistical fantasies? That he was a speed freak? Yeah, I guess you did find out a lot."

His last line was thrown away with excruciating sarcasm.

"Everything you're saying now, Tony, I

thought yesterday when I got back. But there is another way to look at it, a way that could very well mean the NYPD doesn't know what it is talking about."

He leaned forward, the sarcasm gone. He began to tap a staccato beat on the desk. He was very interested but he wanted to retain his cool. That was Tony. I found myself looking at him suddenly with enormous affection. Why hadn't Tony and I ever slept together? Why hadn't we become lovers? He was a dear, sad, crazy, talented man. So what if he was married? Why hadn't I taken that final step? I was very lonely. I knew there was no promise of love unless one initiated it . . . unless one fought for it. Was I happy with my career as a priestess of avant-garde theater? It was profoundly fake. There were few plays and fewer parts that interested me. My cats indeed were beloved by me, but even they could not fill the widening hole in my life. What was the matter with me? He was there . . . willing . . . eager . . . waiting. To him I was always beautiful, cryptic, intelligent—his erotic theatrical fantasy. Why not?

Then I pushed all that nonsense out of my head. I could think about it later. Now there was work to do.

"I now think, Tony, that Bruce Chessler knew he was going to die."

"That's bizarre."

"Not really. Follow me carefully on this. Try to look at it the way his grandmother used to look at character development in a role. Remember? The part is within you, no matter how different the role is from your-self. It will come out real only if your emo-tions are real."

"Shit, Swede, is this a Method class in how to play Bruce Chessler?"

"Sort of, Tony. Bear with me. Suppose you had a dog . . . a much-loved dog."

"Okay."

"Now, under what circumstances would you give your dog away?"

"None."

"What about if you lost your job?"

"No."

"If you got kicked out of your apartment?"

"No."

"If you were sick?"

"No, Swede, under no circumstances."

"Except one."

"Which is?"

"If you knew you were going to die."

"Well, that's about the only one."

"Right. So I think, Tony, that Bruce Chess-ler knew he was going to die, so he gave his cats away."

Basillio got off his chair and began to pace, peering out toward the machines from time to time as if to let his employees know that while he was indeed entertaining a tall hand-some woman in his office, he, the entrepre-neurial genius behind Mother Courage Copying Shops, was on the case.

Then he patted me on the head in a hu-morously patronizing manner, as if I were a gifted child who was also a disciplinary problem. Then he sat back down in his swivel chair.

"So what else is new, Swede?"

"There's more, Tony. It is because he felt he was going to die that he was able to confess his love for me. Before then, he could only write letters that he could not mail."

"Look, Swede, what you're saying is possible. But only barely possible. And, if so, so what? Maybe he had screwed some drug supplier and knew he was going to get shot."

"Then why would he show up for the meeting? No, Tony, that doesn't wash. From all accounts of the murder, there was an amicable meeting in the bar, then a sudden argument, and then shots fired. He didn't go to the bar that night thinking a drug supplier was going to murder him."

"Then who did he think was going to abort his short, glorious life, Swede?"

"I haven't the slightest idea," I admitted.

"So what do we do?"

"Well, first of all, we have to track down or understand his pet hates . . . or at least the hates his girlfriend identified."

"Which are?"

"His grandmother."

"Who's dead."

"Right. And three of her émigré colleagues. The girl Risa mentioned Bukai, Chederov, and Mallinova."

He repeated the names like they were lyrics of a song.

"I thought maybe, Tony, you could take the afternoon off tomorrow and come with me to the Lincoln Center Library of the Performing Arts.

"Why not, Swede? What else do successful businessmen have to do on afternoons other than manufacture erotic fantasies?"

"Bless you, Tony," I said, kissing him lightly on the cheek before I walked out. My legs were trembling and I had a ferocious desire to brush my long hair.

We met by the pool with the Henry Moore sculpture—in front of the Vivian Beaumont Theater at Lincoln Center. Basillio stretched out languorously on one of the stone benches.

"I think we should go in and get to work," I said.

"There's time," he replied.

He kept refusing to go in and I kept getting more and more impatient, more and more nudging.

"Well, you might as well know the truth, Swede; I am enjoying sitting here because it is on this very bench that yours truly, Anthony Basillio, stage designer par excellence, theatrical philosopher, Brechtian scholar—it was right here in either 1976 or 1977 that I gave up theater and became a goddamn capitalist."

"I thought people gave up the theater in bars."

"How would you know, Swede? You never gave it up," he retorted happily; then he swung his feet over the side and we walked into the library, which specializes in theater, film, dance, music, and allied fields.

Within a half-hour after entering, we had requisitioned an entire table and piled it high with sources—collections of theatrical reviews bound and unbound . . . biographical directories of theater people . . . histories of the New York theater and the Russian theater and the world theater.

What we found was this. Lev Bukai, Nikolai Chederov, and Pyotr Mallinova were all members of the Moscow Art Theater up to the 1920s, when they all, at one time or another, left Moscow and went into exile. They all ended up eventually in New York by the late 1940s, where their colleague Maria Swoboda was living and was about to become a respected drama coach because of her association with Stanislavski and his Method.

In the late 1950s they all banded together to form a repertory company—the Nikolai Group—which would continue the tradition of the Moscow Art Theater. Bukai and Chederov were the directors. Mallinova, the producer. Maria Swoboda was on the board and played many character roles. The group traveled throughout the world and was much acclaimed. Its last production in New York was in 1967—Gogol's *Inspector General*—and then it disbanded.

So there it was for what it was worth. We gathered the books and directories and clippings and brought them back to their respective shelves and desks.

Then Basillio and I walked across the street to O'Neal's Balloon and had drinks.

"So what happens now?" he asked as he

played with the large, almost grotesque piece of celery jutting out of his Bloody Mary.

I didn't really know "what happens now," as Basillio put it. The visit to the library had obviously been successful—information-wise. But it had opened up a whole other can of heuristic worms. The oddity of the situation became acute. How and why would a young actor like Bruce Chessler have a contempt for and hatred of people like Bukai, Chederov, Mallinova? It didn't figure. Young actors always hate people who "sell out," who go Hollywood—they hate the hustlers and liars and frauds who seem to infest the theater in all cultures and at all times.

But they rarely hate people like the Russian émigrés from the Moscow Art Theater. These people were truly dedicated, truly important, truly persecuted. These people have always been considered the very best of what the theater had to offer in modern times.

They had been through the whirlwind. They had studied and worked and suffered and triumphed with the great Stanislavski. They were theater people par excellence.

"I think," I said to Basillio, "I'm going to pay a visit to Lev Bukai."

"Why him?"

"Why not?"

"I mean, why not the others?"

"Them too. But first I think I'll pay a visit to Bukai. After all, he was probably the most famous of the émigrés and he was a director of the Nikolai Group—whatever that was."

"Do you want me along?"

"No. Not for the first one. Maybe later."

He pulled the celery stalk out of his Bloody Mary and made as if to fling it across the bar.

"Tony!" I censored him quickly and strongly, then realized he was not going to do it—only faking the throw.

"Still a middle-class schoolmarm at heart, huh, Swede?" he taunted, and I felt stupid.

"That's because no matter how old you get, Tony, you still don't know how to be around women . . . you still must act the difficult child."

"But not as difficult as Bruce Chessler," he noted in response, and suddenly a gloom seemed to descend from the walls and the ceiling and wrap me in despondence. Tony placed a gentle brotherly arm around my shoulder and I let him keep it there.

15

It was very difficult to believe that Lev Bukai lived here. I was standing in front of a magnificent old white-stone building on Ninety-fourth Street just east of Fifth Avenue—the Carnegie Hill section of Manhattan. Where had he gotten all the money to obtain it? The original front had been demolished and replaced with a brick wall and a large burnished oak door that opened directly onto the street. It was like the new owner had decided to build a monastery and then thought better of it. Or maybe after he had moved into the posh neighborhood he realized a monastery wasn't necessary because two blocks away was the main headquarters of the Russian Orthodox persuasion in North America, which housed, among others, the exiled patriarch. Even I knew that, and I'm not Russian Orthodox.

A young woman in a smock answered the door quickly when I twisted the elaborate ringer.

"May I see Lev Bukai?" I asked.

"Who are you?" she countered, obviously not used to having people show up at the front door. She looked like an art-school teacher. Her hair was pulled back severely.

"An old student of Maria Swoboda's," I answered, thinking that it was my connection with the old teacher that would guarantee me an audience. I also made a point of lapsing into the deferential dialect that all the émigrés seemed to require in the student-teacher relationship. One should always, at least metaphorically, bow one's head to one's teacher.

I was right. The name Madame Swoboda was the key. The woman left me at the door with a hushed gesture and returned a minute later, ushering me in.

The place was like a vengeful mausoleum. Huge pieces of old dark furniture soaked up the summer light and seemed to convert it immediately to heat. It felt like it was about two hundred degrees.

Lev Bukai was sitting in what appeared to be a study, although there were no bookcases and the literally thousands of books in the room were piled up on what seemed to be folding tables. Many paintings hung without any sense of balance or composition on the wall. They were portraits of people I didn't know or didn't recognize, done in a heroic style—arms crossed, legs thrust out and apart, jaws jutting, tunics only half-buttoned. And the women were all in languorous poses with enormous heads of brilliant hair.

Lev Bukai looked me up and down. I smiled. He still had that director's eye. He was a tiny, twisted gnome of a man, hidden in a terry-cloth robe. A glass of tea was in his lap. There was no fan or air conditioner in the room.

His nose and ears were bulbous and one eye was partially closed. His blotch-marked skin seemed to have been stretched tight against the bones by a machine.

"So, you knew Maria Swoboda."

"Years ago," I said. I wasn't nervous. But I was frightened by him . . . by the tradition he incarnated. It was, in a sense, like being about to interrogate a Buddha. I realized that I should have brought Basillio. And for the first time in a long while I was very conscious of my dress. I had put on a long skirt with a long-sleeved black cotton jersey. Like a drama student, I realized shamefacedly.

"You were student of hers?"

"Yes."

He grinned, one of those arrogant Russian-émigré grins that say no one from Minnesota will ever understand what they are all talking about.

"She is dead," he noted, running an arthritic hand through what remained of his brushed-back white hair.

"Yes, I know, and I appreciate your seeing me—but it's not about her that I came to see you."

"A part? You want a part?" He laughed uproariously at his own joke.

Then he added: "But I no longer in theater. I'm country gentleman now. Like Oblomov." And he laughed again and then began to cough and choke and wheeze.

Did he really believe that he was in the country? It was a possibility, I thought.

"I want to talk with you, Mr. Bukai, about her grandson."

"Whose grandson?"

"Maria Swoboda's grandson."

He stared at me from beneath a lowered head and sipped the tea in his glass. For the first time since I had entered his home I really felt the power of the old guard—tea from a samovar, dark and pungent, not from a tea bag. This tiny arthritic eighty-five-year-old man in front of me had more theater in one toe than I had in my whole body. And above all, he was European theater in all of its glory and excesses and wanderings and abortions. I remembered how I was literally speechless the first time I met Maria Swoboda—so many years ago. The towering ghost of Stanislavski covered them all like a mantle.

"I don't know that she had grandson," Bukai said. It was obvious he was not going to ask me to sit.

"But surely she must have told you . . . or showed you a picture of him. His name was Bruce Chessler."

"No."

"Did she never speak about him?"

"No. Never."

"And no one else spoke of him?"

"No."

"But she had a grandson," I said to him, frustrated. The back of my jersey was now clinging wetly to my skin.

He nodded his head as if everything were

possible and then went back to his tea. I waited. He said nothing. He stopped looking at me. "Please!" I suddenly blurted out. My plea seemed to infuriate him. He lifted a small table with one straining hand and let it smack into the floor. The young woman was instantly in the room. She stared at me threateningly. Then she ushered me out without another word. The door was slammed behind me.

It was eleven-thirty in the morning. My next stop was Nikolai Chederov. He lived on Seventh Avenue and Fifty-fifth Street in a magnificent landmark apartment house. The doorman wouldn't let me in. He called Chederov on the lobby phone. I shouted into the receiver that I wanted to talk to him about Maria Swoboda's grandson—Bruce Chessler. He said in a very loud voice: "Who?" I repeated myself. "Don't know," he yelled. Then: "You crazy! Go away!" And he hung up. The doorman escorted me out.

Pyotr Mallinova, unlike Bukai and Chederov, had only his phone listed in the phone book—no address. This was odd, because émigrés are always obsessive about listing their full and correct and current names, addresses, and phone numbers in any and every source they can, because one never knows when old friends will suddenly pop up and look for them.

Anyway, I called him from a phone booth on Seventh Avenue and Fifty-seventh Street, right in front of Carnegie Hall. I let the phone ring a long, long time. No one answered. I called a half-hour later. Then another half-hour later. I then began to call every fifteen minutes until I met Basillio, as planned, in a coffee shop in the Village.

Once, during the calls, someone picked up the phone, listened, then hung up.

"I contacted Bukai and Chederov," I told Basillio when we were seated and served, "and neither of them claimed to know anything about Bruce Chessler, much less confirm his existence. Mallinova, I couldn't contact."

"Do you believe them?"

"I don't know. I really don't know."

"Where does this all leave you now? I mean, your theory that Chessler knew he was going to die and that it was something involved with his hatred for those people that did him in rather than a bad drug deal."

"I don't know. I don't know what to think. It was just something to follow up. Like his connection with Arkavy Reynolds. It was just something unique—a young man's bitter hatred for some old people. Don't you think it should have been followed up?" I asked him somewhat tartly.

He grinned and bent over his cup and blew some foam from the top of his capuccino by way of an answer.

"And I'm glad I followed up, because there is something very strange about these Russians."

"What? That they're still alive?"

"Their wealth, I mean. Where did they get the money to live the way they do? They were émigré actors, directors, producers. They were starving like all the others. They never made it to Hollywood like the Germans. Maria Swoboda never seemed to have a dime."

"Swede, that kind of stuff is very hard to find out."

"Why?"

"Remember when we were in the library? The biographical directories don't give information on finances. They tell you about their careers . . . where born . . . where educated . . . who married. That's it."

"What do you suggest?"

"Call their accountants."

"Very funny."

"There probably is a way."

"How?"

"Get someone who really knows these people."

"These people are in their eighties and nineties."

"I mean someone who knows their history, their ties to Stanislavski. I mean someone who knows how they grew and splintered and scattered."

"Fine in theory, Tony, but I don't know anyone like that."

He cocked his head in his infuriating fashion and said slyly: "Oh, yes you do, Swede."

"Don't tell me who I know," I replied angrily. He was beginning to annoy me again. How had I ever contemplated sleeping with him?

"Joseph Grablewski," he said slyly.

I don't know what I looked like at that moment, but I do know that I felt like the blood had drained from my body.

It was a very special, very fearful name from the past.

Grablewski had been one of the bright-shining stars of theatrical criticism in the early 1970s. He used to lecture at the Dramatic Workshop when Basillio and I attended, and I had fallen wildly, crazily in love with him.

And I had done about everything I could think of to get him interested—from the subtle to the exhibitionistic—but he wasn't. It didn't happen.

I could visualize him easily—corduroy jacket, ridiculous tie, face like a large bird's—a hawk or a falcon—and that enormous shock of black-gray hair.

And I could remember that intense, quiet, enfolding, mind-bending way of talking that swept you up into his way of thinking . . . that made you want to think. . . .

He had been a mesmerizing intellectual. He talked about the theater like no one I had ever heard talk about it before. He, above all, had been the reason I decided to cast my lot with the concept of an avant-garde . . . with a concept that no longer existed. He, above all, was the reason I was still supporting myself by cat-sitting at age forty-one—because I simply could not put my art and craft, my brain and heart, at the service of a popular culture I loathed. Or, to put it another way, he had activated my intellectual and theatrical arrogance. I wanted to be immortal—not a movie actress. Grablewski had loved the Russians and their Moscow Art Theater and all theaters caught up in revolutions—real and imagined—and he taught us to love them.

I had been desperately in love with him, and his ignoring of me was, at the time, an enormous tragedy . . . it made me fearful for my life . . . it shattered my sexual self-confidence. Men had always desired me. Why not him?

All I could say in response to Basillio was: "Is he still alive?"

"Alive and crazy and still holding court in that bar on Forty-fourth Street."

"He must be an old man by now," I said.

Basillio grinned at me in response. "Not all that old. And even if he's ninety—so what? If anyone can tell you about secret things in the lives of Bukai, Chederov, and Mallinova, it's him. Right?"

It was nine o'clock that evening. I was standing, believe it or not, in the Forty-fourth Street bar, west of Eighth Avenue, staring through the dim light at the man who sat in a far booth—Joseph Grablewski.

He didn't look much different. His hair was still thick and wild, although all white. He wore the same kind of clothes. He emanated the same kind of nervous energy. And he was drinking the same thing—vodka.

But where were the young people? The actors, actresses, designers, students who used to throng about him? Was he talking to himself now? Was he still talking? What kind of hole had he been in all these years? Why had he become anonymous?

I started walking toward him.

Halfway there, he saw me and began to sing, sardonically: "There she is . . . Miss America."

Suddenly weak, I slid into the booth across from him. His stupid sarcastic song brought back a thousand conflicting memories. My head was like a deranged projection machine.

He smiled at me. His face, up close, had indeed changed—broken down and weary. But the form, the frame, was ageless.

"Do you remember me?" I asked very quickly. I was still shaking a bit.

"Oh, yes . . . oh, yes," he said, leaning back and clasping his hands behind his head as if he were about to make an academic point.

He described his remembering: "The Dramatic Workshop. Many years ago. There she is . . . Miss America. Vaguely beautiful. Vaguely committed. Vaguely talented. Vaguely, vaguely, vaguely."

"Well," I retorted bitterly, "it is better than always being vaguely drunk."

His eyes sparked anger. Then contempt. For whom? Himself? Me? Then he relaxed.

"And you have come to see me because you want to know what happened to the theatrical lion. What happened to my world view. To my criticism. Where are the books? Where are the productions? Where are the insights which dazzle and dazzle?"

"Perhaps." The bar was like a tired, seedy cathedral.

"I became enlightened," he said.

I looked at his vodka glass and at the table in the booth, which seemed not to have been wiped in a decade. I was making a silent point.

"It was all nonsense," he continued, "the theater is all nonsense. Probably has been nonsense since the Greeks."

He sipped his vodka, then drank some Coca-Cola, then lit a cigarette.

"If I remember, also, you tried to get into bed with me. You tried real hard."

"Yes, I did."

"Sorry," he muttered. "I had other agendas at the time. And you probably would have caught a social disease from me. Anyway, in retrospect it was all a mistake. Look how well you've aged."

"Still vaguely beautiful?" I asked, laughing. The laugh seemed to defuse my awe and painful nostalgia.

"Decidedly so."

A waiter came over. I ordered a club soda. Joseph Grablewski ordered another Stolichnaya.

He stared hard at me.

"So, you sought me out once again to verify your original desires. You want to sleep with me. You want to confirm a desire—how long?—fifteen years old. You want a ripe old alkie like myself to share your bed to confirm that at one time in the past you were right—that the theater is of great cosmic importance and that I am/was one of its gurus. You are still in the theater, aren't you? Could you be anywhere else?"

"My name is Alice Nestleton," I said in response, "and the only reason I'm here is to ask you about some Russian-émigré theater people."

"Who?"

"Their names are Bukai, Chederov, and Mallinova."

He laughed hugely, sweeping his arms backward. "A third-rate gallery of Stanislavski clones. God, I haven't heard their names in years. I thought they were all dead."

"And I thought you were dead," I retorted.

"Lev Bukai . . . director of the ill-fated Nikolai Group . . . left the Soviet Union I don't know when . . . in Paris for a few years . . . debacle as dramatic consultant for the old Ballets Russes of Monte Carlo . . . brought to the United States by Hurok in the late forties . . . arrogant retarded son of a bitch."

I was astonished by this alcoholic's almost total recall.

"What about the others?"

"What about them?" He sneered and drank his vodka.

Then he said: "Do you want me to tell you about the productions of the Nikolai Group? . . . Their repertoire? . . . Their special brand of fakery? All fake . . . all those émigrés were fake. They couldn't stand the revolution's heat and its poverty and its demand for real theater, so they left for the usual bullshit—artistic freedom."

He began to laugh so loud I thought he

would fall over. Then he stopped suddenly and stared at me. He reached over and touched me on the side of the face. I pushed his hand away as if it were poisonous. He reached over and touched me again on the face. I let his hand stay there. I wanted it to stay there. It was astonishing, but my old feelings for him were beginning to resurrect themselves.

"How old are you?" I asked him, breaking the spell.

"Sixty-six chronologically . . . one hundred and sixty-one spiritually."

The bizarre thought came to me that I should take him home with me and take care of him and give him some soup and some coffee and then sit down and talk. How I wanted to really talk to him then . . . right then . . . about the theater . . . about the old times . . . about what he knew and why he kept it a secret . . . about why he had pulled into himself and the vodka. The thought frightened me. I was becoming very frightened.

I moved as far away from him as I could in the booth.

"I want to know where Lev Bukai got his money."

"How do you know he has money?"

"I know. I saw his home."

"Why should I tell you?"

"Do I have to give you a reason?"

"Not really. I just want one."

"Because something terrible happened and it may involve him."

"Everyone knows where Bukai got his money."

"Where."

"Diamonds. He's part-owner of a diamond firm. Did you really think he got his town house by producing and directing ridiculous plays by Gogol?"

"What firm?"

"I don't know."

"Please think."

"It was some kind of funny-named firm . . . Syrian or Egyptian. No . . . Turkish. That's what I heard—a firm run by Turks . . . or Turkish Jews."

"Can't you remember?"

"Give me some Turkish names. I'll try."

"I don't know what a Turkish name is."

"Wait," he said, rubbing his nose lightly as if the gesture brought him recall. "It was the same name as a singer . . . an old pop singer. Wait . . . right. Sedaka . . . like the singer Neil Sedaka."

"Thank you," I whispered.

He had given me what I came for. Or had he? I didn't want to leave. I wanted to talk about something else, but words wouldn't come. A feeling of almost unbearable sadness seemed to envelop us. I had the feeling that if we had had an affair—then—everything about our lives would have been different. I would no longer be struggling. He would not be drinking himself to death on Forty-fourth Street. I would not have a history of broken affairs and a broken marriage. Everything would have been different. Even the theater . . . yes . . . even the theater . . . together we would have made a difference.

I was lapsing into megalomania. I couldn't afford it. Bruce Chessler's loud sport shirt seemed to be waving toward me. I had a murder to solve.

"Visit me again," he said softly. I nodded as I left.

16

"I really question the wisdom of this move. We're going over the line, Swede."

We were standing outside the building on Forty-seventh Street that housed Sedaka and Sons, Diamond Merchants. It was a street that had always fascinated me . . . and repelled me. It was so much like the theater. Glittering rocks passed hands for enormous sums. Rational people became obsessed with form and color.

I didn't answer.

"We really can't just walk in there and ask all kinds of questions. They'll kick us out. Listen, Swede. What does this have to do with anything? You have this crazy notion that the kid knew he was going to die. So he gave away his white cats. And now you know that this kid hated old Russian theater people and the ones he hated most turn out to be rich. What the hell does anything have to do with anything?"

"Nothing has to do with anything," I replied, "until you make it."

Basillio groaned. "Are you going to give me a goddamn lecture on the philosophical aspects of criminal investigation? Don't! It's

ten-thirty in the morning and already eighty-
one degrees. Besides, I don't care anything
about criminal investigation as a branch of
philosophy."

"Are you coming?" I asked, making plain
to him that I wouldn't be surprised if he
didn't.

He followed me, grumbling, into the lobby
and up in the elevator to the third floor.

A receptionist who was wearing a beautiful
blue silk dress refused us admittance at first.
What is your business? Personal, I replied.
Not good enough, she said. Please leave or I'll
call security. On and on it went like that.
Back and forth. Predictable. Basillio was becoming very embarrassed. We were receiv-
ing ugly stares from other people in the
reception area, several of them carrying those
small strange leather cases under the arm.
Diamonds, no doubt.

Finally I said: "Please tell Mr. Sedaka that
we wish to speak with him privately—about
Lev Bukai."

They were truly magic words. A minute
later a heavyset man of about fifty, with a
thick mustache and wearing a beautifully
tailored silk suit, white shirt, and silk tie,
stepped outside and beckoned for us to follow him into his office. Silk seemed to be the
motif of this milieu. Diamonds and silk.

We followed. He pointed out the two chairs
we should sit on and then slid himself behind
a large, totally empty desk.

"What is this all about, now?" he asked,
obviously annoyed and not hiding it, staring

first at me and then at Basillio and then from one to the other as if he couldn't really decide who was the real culprit.

Basillio was squirming. He didn't understand . . . he could never understand that one must follow each strand back to the center no matter how absurd the strand seemed . . . or how far away the center appeared.

I jumped in. "I want to know what kind of relationship exists, if any, between Lev Bukai and your firm."

"That's none of your business."

"I would appreciate your cooperation in this matter."

"Who the hell are you, lady?" he exploded.

"The ghost of Christmas past," I replied. It was odd, but I felt no sense of being intrusive. I was where I was supposed to be.

"Oh, God," I heard Basillio moan.

The man across the desk stared at me for a long time, as if making an evaluation; as if trying to decide whether I was a cop or an insurance investigator or a bill collector or a plain lunatic.

He seemed to be evaluating the price of his silence. He seemed to be running through options. The longer he remained silent, the more he implicated himself.

Then he gave a great wrenching sigh and said: "Lev Bukai has been a silent partner in this firm's start, its development, and its success. And he was a very close friend of my late father, who founded the firm. I have met Mr. Bukai maybe twice in my life. I really have no contact with him whatsoever."

He waited for my response. I felt a sense of triumph. He had told me what I wanted to know. What it meant didn't really matter. The knowledge was sufficient. Grablewski had been confirmed.

"I want to thank you for your help, Mr. Sedaka," I said. "I doubt if I will bother you again."

And then we were out of his office as quickly as we had entered, whisking ourselves out as if our bodies would leave telltale stains on the furniture. Basillio and I walked east on Forty-seventh Street until we reached Fifth Avenue.

"So," he said finally, bursting, "what the hell does it prove? Three Russian émigrés come to the promised land and parlay their hard-earned cash into what turns out to be a winner—the diamond merchant named Sedaka. It's the goddamn American dream. What does it all have to do with that poor dead fool named Bruce Chessler—who, by the way, hated them and his grandmother? Really, what does it have to do with anything?"

I put my fingers to my lips for a moment, to shut him up.

"Did anything seem strange about him, Tony?"

"Yeah, it was strange he didn't kick us out on our asses."

"I mean about his appearance . . . his face in particular."

"No."

"Didn't you notice that his jaw seemed to be lighter in color than the rest of his face?"

"No, I didn't. Maybe he forgot to turn over when he went to the Bahamas. Maybe his window is striped from dirt and the sun hits his face in stages."

"It was as if," I continued, ignoring his analysis, "he had worn a beard for a long time and then recently shaved it. The skin under the beard, once exposed, would be lighter than the rest of his face."

"So what?"

"The detectives told me they have a description of the man who murdered Bruce Chessler—a heavyset man with a beard, about fifty."

"Sure," said Basillio sardonically, "and he also deals in speed when he's not cutting diamonds." He kissed me quickly and hailed a cab. He had to play the boss.

I walked home. It was a very strange walk. I kept thinking about Bruce Chessler and Clara and all the peculiar connections which continued to arise surrounding them. But something else kept intruding—Joseph Grablewski.

His—Grablewski's—contempt for the three émigrés had been total and relentless, in much the same way Bruce Chessler's had been, at least according to his girlfriend. And there was a wide gulf between what I and others I knew thought about the old émigrés and what Grablewski and Chessler thought of them. How could the émigrés have earned such widely varied judgments on their lives and time and art? Just because they invested in diamond companies? It was all very strange.

My thinking about Grablewski was becoming more and more intense. I was determined not to go to that bar again. Why should I? But I knew I would go there. I would go there again, I would talk to him again, I would sit in that booth again, directly across from him. I silently cursed Basillio for telling me where I could find him . . . for reminding me that he would have the information I needed.

I finally reached my block and house and began to climb the stairs. Bushy had been sulking lately because of my irregular hours, and I had planned to bring him a goody. I was at the third landing before I remembered, but I wasn't about to go back down and up. Next time, Bushy, I promised him silently.

"Thank God you're here," a voice suddenly yelled out at me as I reached the final landing.

I cringed at the sudden loud noise and shrank back when a figure seemed to materialize out of nowhere—just as Bruce Chessler had appeared that night.

"Don't you remember me?" the figure yelled again—her voice seemed on the cusp of lunacy.

When my sudden fear vanished I knew quite well who it was—Risa, the girl who had been Bruce Chessler's on-and-off lover.

"Calm down, calm down," I said to the obviously hysterical girl. Then she burst into tears and started to tremble so hard that I grabbed her shoulders.

With great difficulty I got her into the apartment, onto the sofa. She had trouble breathing . . . and then would be fine and speak a whole sentence or two . . . and then become incoherent again and gasp for breath.

Finally she calmed down and sat on the sofa like a rag doll, her punk hair sadly askew, her arms strangely dangling.

She started to explain in a singsong voice: "I was in my apartment on East Fifth Street, listening to some music. I live on the ground floor. I don't know why, but I suddenly looked up and a man standing outside the window started to shoot. There was glass flying all over and my things were breaking and I was sure I was going to die."

She stopped and looked around as if she finally realized she was in a strange apartment.

"I think it has something to do with Bruce. I don't know why. But I know it. And I remembered you and thought you could help me . . . keep me safe . . . so I brought you some of Bruce's stuff . . . what he kept with him all the time . . . or that he kept at my apartment because when he was popping pills and drinking he used to get so paranoid."

I told her to relax, that she was safe with me, that she could stay as long as she wanted.

I made her some iced tea and showed her where to shower; her clothes were drenched with sweat and smelled of her fear.

After she had showered and drunk and

eaten a little she was much calmer and she opened the creased envelope she had brought with her and laid the items out on my rug. Bushy investigated them, found them harmless, and walked away. Pancho flew by them so swiftly he didn't even notice them.

But I noticed them. They were fascinating.

It was a collection of old programs from the Nikolai Group . . . programs of their performances in Central and South America—Mexico City, Rio, Panama City, Managua, Maracaibo, Caracas, Concepción, Quito, and dozens of others, large and small.

"He always studied them," she said, "always, and wrote all over them and . . ."

I knelt on the floor to study them more closely, and she stopped talking.

Bruce Chessler had written obscenities all over the programs in black and red and purple Magic Markers.

There was something about the Nikolai Group that had obviously engaged and infuriated him even more than the individual émigrés.

I stood up and sat down on the sofa alongside Risa, staring at the strange assemblage of old programs.

"What do you think it means?" Risa asked, now obviously convinced by the bullets fired into her apartment that there was something more to her boyfriend's murder than little green pills . . . now ready to reexamine even the most trivial objects.

"I don't know," I replied.

We sat in silence for some time.

"Did you love him?" I asked.

"Who knows? I think so. But he was hard to be with. It was not warm or close with him. Do you know what I mean—it wasn't warm?"

I nodded, reached down and picked Bushy up. Holding him right then, for some reason, made me think of Joseph Grablewski again, and I dropped poor Bushy onto the rug like he was diseased. He was very insulted.

When I looked at Risa again, she was fast asleep. I knew what I had to do next—pay closer attention to Bukai, Chederov, and Mallinova.

As for her, she was one of those child-woman enigmas who seem to haunt the city from generation to generation. She was a cipher. No matter what she told me about herself, I knew nothing. Her sands were always shifting. This year punk . . . next year wholesome . . . the following year demipunk. Doomed to insubstantial change.

17

Lev Bukai exited from his magnificent dwelling at about ten-thirty in the morning. I had been waiting since nine, having decided that surveillance was my only logical move. There was nothing else I could think of. My wait was eased by the knowledge that Basillio was also waiting—for Chederov. Risa had agreed to follow Mallinova, but we could never find out where he lived.

Bukai moved very slowly toward Fifth Avenue, so slowly it seemed the sidewalk was moving instead of him. He carried a yellow cane and he was dressed much too warmly for the late-August weather—a jacket and tie. He crossed over to the park side and entered Central Park at Ninetieth Street, where the horse path meets the reservoir.

Then he began a painfully slow walk down the east side of the park to the sailboat pond, where he finally settled himself down on a bench and watched.

I seated myself on a small grass-covered hill about fifty yards from the beach. I could see him but he could not see me.

He dozed and woke and dozed and woke again. He shifted the cane from one hand to

the other. He smiled at the small boats in the
water, at passing nannies with their baby
carriages, at dog walkers. He seemed totally
at peace with the world.

I should have brought a book along, I realized. The sun and the heat and the bucolic
milieu were making me sleepy.

He sat on that bloody bench for three and
a half hours. Then he stood up, stretched,
and began the laborious walk back to his
house. I followed. By the time he reached his
door he seemed totally exhausted and the
young woman whom I had met earlier had to
come outside and help him in. It was obvious
Lev Bukai was not going out again this day.
I went back to my apartment.

When I opened the door I was startled to
see Risa on the carpet, poring over one of my
old scrapbooks.

She looked up, embarrassed, and explained: "I got the chills, so I looked in your
closet for a wrap and found this. I hope you
don't mind." She looked very cute and vulnerable and apologetic and I didn't mind at
all. I had invited her to stay with me as long
as she was frightened and she could do what
she liked.

"I didn't know you were so famous," she
said.

I laughed. "That was in Minnesota," I explained. "I was the Minnesota actress who
was going to come to New York and rock it
on its heels with my interpretations of deep
parts . . . big parts . . . significant parts. It

didn't happen. I basically have become a star in the cat-sitting world.''

She went back to the scrapbook. I made myself a small salad with cottage cheese and took it into the living room to eat.

"Did you find out anything?'' she asked.

"Well, I found out that Mr. Bukai likes to watch toy boats for hours.''

"You know, this is really very exciting. I once saw a movie about Murder Incorporated. Do you think these old men have a gang? A murder gang? Is that why you are following them? Do you think they murdered Bruce?''

Her kind of buoyant, naïve enthusiasm startled me.

"Where are you from originally, Risa?''

"Maplewood, New Jersey.''

"Where is that?'' I asked. The name of the town seemed vaguely familiar. But maybe there had been a town called Maplewood in Minnesota.

"Oh, out there,'' she said, obviously not interested in pursuing her geography any further. She went back to the scrapbook. I could see her staring at a large picture of me in *The Trojan Women* during my first season with the Tyrone Guthrie Regional Theater. Ah, what a star I was!

"Did Basillio call?'' I asked.

"The phone didn't ring at all when you were gone.''

"You sure? I was also expecting a call from a Mrs. Gordon about a weekend cat-sitting assignment.''

"Wait," she admitted, "the phone did ring but I couldn't get to it in time . . . I had fallen asleep . . . so I thought I would put on the answering machine, but I didn't know how to work it . . . and so—"

I stopped her with my hand. It was okay. Did she want anything to eat? She jumped up, flew to the kitchen, and came back with what was left of the cottage cheese in its container and a soup spoon. We ate together and stared at Bushy, who was staring at us because he liked cottage cheese. Pancho flew by only once and flicked his half-tail at us like we were flies.

"Doesn't he ever stop running?" Risa asked incredulously.

" 'Stop and die' is Pancho's motto," I explained. She shook her head sadly.

By five Basillio still hadn't called. Risa had fallen asleep over the scrapbook.

I felt a sudden need to walk quickly, to stretch my legs, to get out of confinement. I went out of the apartment, down the steps, and onto the street. I began to walk uptown.

At Thirty-fourth Street I stopped. The streets were black with people leaving work. Only there and then could I admit to myself where I was going—to that bar on Forty-fourth Street.

I wanted to see Joseph Grablewski. The realization shocked me at first but then made good clear sense. It seemed the logical thing to do. Like the surveillance. The thought came to me that I was beginning to confuse desire and logic. If so, it was pathetic. I pushed the problem out of my mind.

The bar was crowded. Once inside the coolness and the dimness, I wondered if the long day in the sun watching Lev Bukai had given me a sunstroke. Was that why I was in the bar?

Joseph Grablewski was sitting in the same booth, wearing the same clothes, drinking the same drink. He stared dimly, as if someone was seated opposite him. I walked quickly to the booth and slid in beside him—not across from him like the last time, but beside him. My shoulder was touching his. I could smell him—a mixture of vodka and sweat and anxiety . . . a desperate smell.

"What is the matter?" he asked. His fake solicitousness enraged me for some reason or another.

"The matter? Nothing's the matter with me. It's with you," I yelled, and my hand hit his vodka glass so that it slid across the table and upended.

Then I started to cry. And I started to babble. About Bushy and Pancho. About my class in the New School. About the old scrapbook that Risa was looking over. About my desperate need for a part, a real part. I was talking about theater . . . about what I loved . . . and I talked about my last lover, the horse trainer . . . and the last murder I had solved, of that wonderful demonic old man Harry Starobin . . . and I talked about curtain calls and scripts and makeup . . . back and forth I babbled and then, exhausted, turned to face

him as I pressed myself against his chest,
fiercely, as if we were lovers, as if by doing
that I could erase the past fifteen years . . . or
bring him back his mind.

Without looking at him, I let my hand run
over his face. But it wasn't an old face my
fingers felt; it was a young face; and it wasn't
the face of Grablewski—it was the face of
Bruce Chessler.

My God! I pushed myself away from the
man and stood up. People were beginning to
stare at me. The waiter started to walk over.
I ran out. I needed to rest. I needed to gather
my forces and talk to my cats. The investigation of the three old men was beginning to
unravel me, but nothing yet had happened to
do so . . . not one single thing . . . not one solitary juncture. It was all objects in space: diamonds, theatrical programs, white cats,
punk girls, wealthy émigrés. All, as Grablewski had said, lackluster clones of Stanislavski.

18

Basillio lasted seven days on surveillance before he resigned in disgust. He told me the old man he was watching went around the block twice a day and that was it, except on Saturday, when he walked to Bloomingdale's and bought a tie, and on Sunday, when he went to the D'Agostino on Fifty-seventh and Ninth to shop. Since we never found where Mallinova lived, that left me alone, doggedly waiting for Bukai to emerge each day. I began, in fact, to welcome the drudgery because it kept me from any further lunatic forms of behavior vis-à-vis Joseph Grablewski.

I kept on. I was dogged. I would follow the strands to the center just as Bruce Chessler had followed them to his death. That it kept me from Grablewski was no doubt important—I wanted to get control of that escalating danger . . . a pathetic attempt to escalate an old unrequited love. And the worst delusion of all—that there was some relationship between Bruce Chessler, the boy who loved me, and Joseph Grablewski, the man I had once loved as desperately and futilely. Oh, there were so many strands now—Arkavy

Reynolds, diamonds, speed, white cats, theatrical contradictions. So many . . .

My doggedness paid off on the second
Tuesday in September.

Bukai left the house, crossed Fifth Avenue,
but did not enter the park. Instead he
boarded a downtown bus, with myself five
passengers behind him. He rode all the way
downtown, got off at Eighth Street, walked
through Washington Square Park onto La
Guardia Place, south on La Guardia Place to
Bleecker, and then turned west on Bleecker.

It was a long, arduous walk for the old man,
but he kept it up. Finally he turned off
Bleecker and into a coffeehouse—Café Vivaldi—a wonderful place I had been many
times.

I waited across the street. He did not re-
emerge. So I crossed over and sat down in
the sidewalk-café section of the coffeehouse.
From where I sat I could see Bukai's head
through the window.

But he was not alone. Two other old men
sat with him. I knew who they were instantly: Chederov and Mallinova. The words
of that punk girl, Risa, came chillingly back
to me: a Murder Incorporated of old men. But
who really knew what they were doing there?

They ordered coffee and exotic pastries and
I could dimly hear that they were talking in
what had to be Russian.

I ordered an espresso and sipped it, watching the street, listening to the sounds from
inside.

A man passed, walking a dog. He smiled at

me. I smiled back, broadly. I was happy. My speculations had been confirmed. I had postulated that the three old men were not random hates of Bruce Chessler's, that they were a unit, a set, that whatever existed in their group or in their relation to others could only be understood because they were acting or not acting in concert. There had been other members of the Nikolai Group, but only these three had garnered Bruce Chessler's almost lunatic hate—and only these three were relevant now. At least to the young man's death.

The man walking the dog crossed the street, holding the leash tightly. I started to speculate as to why dog people make good street cops, for example, but only cat people make good investigative detectives. It had to do with the interpretation of behavior. With dogs, everything was hands-on or paws-on. The dog wagged his tail, licked your face. You put him on a leash, hit him with a paper, soothed him with a bone, scratched his head.

With cats it was different. To know your cat's feelings or to interpret its behavior, you had to rely on clues, on interpretations of past facts and past complexes of facts, none of which were mathematically precise.

My musings were interrupted by the sound of scraping chairs. Why was the meeting being adjourned?

What had the émigrés agreed or disagreed about? What had they been discussing? Were they twisted assassins or were they lovable old men?

Mallinova left first; then Chederov. Bukai remained seated, but I could see he was paying the bill. I left my payment on the outside table and waited across the street.

After he exited, Bukai began to walk slowly through the streets, finally ending up on Hudson Street. He walked two more blocks downtown and then vanished into a store.

It was a pet store. Maybe he's buying a turtle, I thought, to accompany him on his walks.

I peered into the window. The front part of the store carried specialized dog bones, exotic cans of cat food, leashes and mufflers and all kinds of pet paraphernalia, ranging from the practical to the absurd.

Deeper into the store were the cages. It was obviously a place that boarded dogs and cats as well as sold them.

I could see Bukai in the rear section staring into one of the cages.

My antenna—or whatever it was between my actress's ears—began to pulsate.

He could be in the store, I realized, for a number of reasons, and at least two of them might be most interesting.

When he came out, I was faced with a dilemma. If I kept following him, I wouldn't be able to go into the store. If I went into the store, I would lose him.

I went into the store. A young man with a bright red bow tie and baggy pants asked me if I needed help. I told him I was just looking.

I spent about five minutes staring at a gray parrot in a large cage with a price tag of $741.

Would my cats like it? As a friend? As a meal?

Then I slowly meandered to the rear, where the beasties were boarded and sold.

"Clara," I screamed, not able to contain myself when I saw the large white cat with the black-spotted rump and face in the cage. She regarded me coolly.

The young man in the red bow tie looked at me with severe disapproval for my outburst.

The trouble was, there were three Claras in three separate cages! It was an astonishing sight. I started to giggle crazily. Then I got hold of myself.

Why not? I thought. One was my Clara. The other two were the cats given to Risa and then taken.

I could see that Bukai had brought them some tidbits.

Only one of the Claras was eating the gift.

A sudden calm came over me as I basked in the safety of Clara and her friends. I was beginning to perceive a pattern. I was beginning to close the circle . . . to pull the strands closer to the center.

"Are you looking for a kitten?" the young man asked, smelling a purchase.

"Not right now," I said, and quickly walked out of the store.

19

It was ten A.M. the next day. I was having my second cup of coffee and treasuring the events and revelations of the previous day. Risa had decided that during her last few days with me she would make herself useful—so she was running up and down the stairs to the washing machines and dryers in the basement, carrying pillow cases full of supposedly dirty clothes. I had the feeling that she was wreaking havoc by throwing some things of mine into a machine that simply should not have been there. But her instincts and intent were so good and so refreshing that I didn't have the heart to intervene even to ask a question. Let her ruin a few things, I thought.

Then Basillio called. His voice was low, clinical.

"Grablewski is in the hospital, Swede, and I heard it's bad. He collapsed in that bar last night, or yesterday afternoon."

"What's the matter with him?"

"I don't know. Like I said, all I heard was that he collapsed and was taken to Beth Israel."

I was silent on the phone. The phone receiver seemed odd to me, like it shouldn't be capable of transmitting sound. Inside of me there were all kinds of turmoil, but nothing came out. The thought that Joseph Grablewski was in pain was almost unbearable to me. It made me mute.

"Do you want to see him?" Basillio asked kindly when my silence persisted.

"Yes," I whispered.

"Wait there," Basillio said, bless him, and hung up the phone.

A half-hour later Basillio and I stood at a reception desk in one of the small wings of Beth Israel's alcoholism ward. We circled each other nervously, waiting for a Dr. Wallace.

He arrived in ten minutes or so, a very tall, stooped man who looked about seventy-five. He had bulging eyes and glasses that were perched on his forehead.

"Who are you?" he demanded, unfriendly, impatient, skeptical.

"Friends of his. Can we see him?" I asked.

He shrugged mightily and moved off, gesturing with one hand that we should follow. We passed through an open door and then a locked door and came to a ward divided into small cubicles of two beds each.

Dr. Wallace stopped in front of one. He pointed. I stared at the figure on the bed. It looked like a dead man. Grablewski was lying on his back, his arms strangely folded, as if he had just emerged out of some kind of restraint. His body was absolutely pale . . . like some fiend had drained his blood. I could see that he was breathing; his chest cage was moving. His eyes were half-open but not focusing. He looked childlike on that bed. The sight of him made me weak. I grasped the end of the steel cot. Basillio reached out to steady me but didn't make contact.

"What happened to him?" I asked plaintively.

"Are you kidding me? I thought you were his friend," Dr. Wallace said, his voice stacked with contempt. His response confused me.

"If you're his friend," he continued, "you know he's an alcoholic, don't you? And you know he's been an alcoholic a long time."

There was silence. We were all standing, not speaking, and seeming at cross-purposes.

"Okay, ladies and gentlemen," Dr. Wallace said in a resigned, sardonic voice, "let me give you the lesson you crave. The gentleman you are looking at is suffering from a common condition called fasting alcoholic hypoglycemia. It is usually seen in malnourished alcoholics. It is characterized by conjugate deviation of the eyes, extensor rigidity of the extremities, unilateral or bilateral Babinski reflexes, convulsions, transient hemiparesis, trismus hypothermia. It is caused by a multifactorial inhibition of gluconeogenesis by ethanol—booze. Your friend was brought here in a comatose state and given glucose intravenously. He is coming around quite nicely."

Dr. Wallace, having finished his bewildering exposition, nodded and then left. He stopped once and called back: "By the way, only about eleven percent of untreated cases of this syndrome die. So don't worry too much about your friend."

There were other humans on other cots, but I felt totally alone with Joseph Grablewski.

I pulled a steel folding chair close to the cot and sat down. I was twelve inches from his face. It was sad . . . so indescribably sad. I was suffused with all kinds of bizarre guilt . . . as if somehow by *not* doing something I had put him there. *Not* become lovers? When? Years ago? Or now?

"Look, he's come to, he recognizes you," Basillio said. The patient's eyes were indeed flickering and he moved one of his arms down by his side. I noticed that there were tremors in his fingers and his tongue flicked in and out of the side of his mouth as if on a desperate search for water.

"He's trying to speak to you, Swede. Go closer to him, he's trying to say something."

Yes, I could see that. I could see that he wanted to speak to me. It made me ambivalent. I wanted to be close to him . . . I wanted to run away. His plight was threatening me. His alcoholism sickened me.

I touched him tentatively, on the hand, like he was a dying man and my gesture made me ashamed.

Then I pressed my lips to his head and whispered, "I'm glad you'll be okay."

He nodded feebly and twisted his head oddly.

"He wants to tell you something," Basillio said. "Put your ear by his mouth."

I did so and waited. I heard sounds but no words. Then, finally, he said something to me that I could retrieve. Then he seemed to collapse and lose consciousness.

We walked out of the ward and onto the street. We stood there watching the traffic, watching the people enter and leave.

"What did he say to you?" Basillio asked.

"It was something odd. He doesn't know what he's saying."

"What?" Basillio was insistent.

"He said . . . no, he asked: Did Constantin bite you?"

Basillio laughed. "He was making fun of you. He remembered when you had asked him about those three Stanislavski disciples. Constantin was Stanislavski's first name."

"I'm aware of his first name, Tony, it's just that I don't think Joseph Grablewski was making some kind of joke."

"Then what does it mean?"

"He was trying to tell me something."

"Oh, come on, Swede, the man is in an alcoholic stupor."

I had to be careful. I didn't want to make a fool of myself in front of Basillio or anyone else when I discussed Joseph Grablewski. Even in a stupor the man upset me. He upset me . . . not his words. I had only a low-level buzz over "Did Constantin bite you?" Low-level but persistent, like an aching molar.

"If he wasn't making a joke, then who is Constantin?"

"Is there a vodka called Constantin?" I asked Basillio.

"I don't think so. At least I've never heard of that brand. Maybe Grablewski thinks he's Stanislavski."

"No, Tony, Grablewski knows he's Grablewski, that's his trouble."

"Well, look, Swede, I gotta get back to work. I'm sure your old friend will be okay. I'll be in touch."

"Thanks, Tony," I said, and watched him walk downtown quickly, heading toward one of his copy shops.

I didn't go anywhere. I just lounged in front of the hospital. Grablewski's stupid whispered comment was like a delayed-action fuse. When I'd first heard it, the words were meaningless. When I discussed it with Basillio, they began to nudge me. And now that I was alone, they were beginning to fester. What was he talking about? Did he mean Stanislavski? Bite me? Had I suffered some kind of attack or setback?

Maybe he was talking about another man called Constantin. Maybe he was talking about a place. Maybe he was talking about a bar called Constantin. Or maybe he didn't even know he was talking to me; maybe he thought he was talking to one of his drinking companions.

I could not leave that stupid phrase alone. Maybe it was the residue of unrequited love. I could not leave it alone. Watch it fester, Alice, I thought to myself. I walked to the corner and stared at the hospital. Poor man . . .

locked in there . . . people sticking things into his arm . . . people restraining him when he got violent—and all so that he could crawl back to that booth on Forty-fourth Street and start all over again.

What was Constantin? Who was Constantin? Where was Constantin? What did the whispered words mean? Then, fifteen minutes after I left the hospital, I was headed uptown in a cab—my destination the same Lincoln Center Library of the Performing Arts that I had visited a short time ago with Basillio.

I knew exactly where to look now for memoirs and histories of the Moscow Art Theater. But this time I wasn't looking for references to Bukai, Chederov, and Mallinova. I was looking for a single reference to a single name—Constantin.

But all I could find were references to Constantin Stanislavski. No, I was sure it was another Constantin. I had the odd feeling as I flipped through the indexes that Joseph Grablewski was somewhere in the massive library, laughing at me, mocking me, guzzling his vodka.

And then, in a single beat-up book published in English in 1948 by a Russian-émigré actor named Orlov, I found the indexed reference: "Constantin, cat."

It was on page 131 of the very bitter memoir.

On that page Orlov recounted how Stanislavski was presented with a white cat named after him by his associates and this cat became a company favorite, not the least because it tended to bite.

I started to laugh right there in the library, so loudly and with such abandon that one of the guards came over and asked me if I could moderate my behavior.

It was impossible, so I had to run out of the library and calm down by the Henry Moore statue. It was bizarre and funny; imagine a line of white cats that began with a cat given to Stanislavski—and now sixty years later at least one of its progeny named Clara and two unknown siblings are hidden in a boarding pet store on Hudson Street after having been kidnapped by Bruce Chessler and then stolen back. And they are brought goodies by an eighty-five-year-old émigré. But why would Chessler have kidnapped the cats in the first place?

The whole thing was crazy. Grablewski was crazy. And for all I knew, Bukai was crazy.

By the time I got home, I was totally exhausted. Risa had gone out and left me a note that she would be back in the late afternoon or early evening. I told Bushy and Pancho about the mysterious line of white cats . . . if indeed such a line existed.

When I had finally showered and eaten and napped, I realized that I ought to at least follow up Grablewski's clue. I pulled out the old programs from the Nikolai Group's travels that Bruce Chessler had so lunatically defaced with his obscenities and carefully went through them searching for something Chessler might have written about Constantin the cat or Clara the cat or any white cat—past, present, or future.

There was no such annotation. It was odd. If Chessler was so obsessed with the émigrés, he must have known that there existed some kind of émigré saying with a double entendre: "Constantin bite you?" There had to be such a saying, or else how could Joseph Grablewski know about it? And surely Chessler's grandmother must have known about it and said something to her grandson about Constantin, Stanislavski's cat.

Well, one couldn't force things. If it wasn't there, it wasn't there.

Going through those old programs made me very sad. All those performances done and gone and forgotten. All those people in all those plays in all capacities—gone.

I smiled as I saw the name of Maria Swoboda, my old teacher, so prominently displayed in the programs. And the pictures the émigrés had used! They were all so heroic! More like the photos of operatic tenors.

I began to feel very reverently toward them. I started to stack them by date.

In 1957 they had gone to Mexico City.

In 1958 to Ecuador.

In 1959 to Panama and Argentina.

In 1960 to Venezuela.

In 1961 to Nicaragua.

In 1962 to Brazil and Costa Rica.

In 1963 to El Salvador.

In 1964 to Chile.

In 1965 to Venezuela.

In 1966 to Peru.

In 1967 to Mexico City and Brazil.

After I had stacked them by date, I realized it was very strange that the Nikolai Group had never performed in Europe, only in South and Central America.

I suddenly became furious at myself for not having studied or even looked at the programs seriously before.

There were many other peculiar facts about the Nikolai Group that emerged after one studied the programs.

For example, in most of the years of their existence they made only one foreign trip each year—to one city in one country.

This was very strange. No other theatrical group I was ever attached to did that. Small groups have to perform many times in many places in the shortest period of time in order to recoup their expenses. The Nikolai Group seemed to make command performances as if they were the Bolshoi Ballet—which they assuredly weren't. How could they have afforded to fly to Buenos Aires, for example, and play in one theater for three nights and then fly back? What was the point artistically, anyway, forget financially?

And there was something even stranger. In the years when they had visited two countries on the same trip, these countries were far apart. This also was unheard-of. European companies, for example, when they came to America to play New York and Boston and Washington, and perhaps Atlanta, always tried to schedule some performances in Montreal, because it was geographically feasible. They wouldn't schedule Kingston, Jamaica.

The itinerary of the Nikolai Group was in some way profoundly fake!

I was so excited at what I had discovered about the programs that I started to pirouette about the living room with joy, until I realized that I wouldn't even have picked up the programs again if the alcoholic Mr. Grablewski hadn't whispered a cryptic comment in my ear.

But the seven strands were indeed beginning to point toward a center. There were Constantin and his progeny—poor Clara. There was a surly diamond merchant. There was a theatrical group that seemed to have defied theatrical logic. There was a murdered young man obsessed by hatred. There were three ancient wealthy émigrés who met from time to time. There was an eccentric bohemian who had been a police informer before he was murdered. And the seventh strand was unrequited love—Chessler's for me, and mine, at one time in the past, for Grablewski. For the first time since that young man had appeared on my landing I could see dimly toward the center—where the strands were leading.

Oh, I had work to do—a lot of work—and some mice to catch. But I knew what I was going to do and I was quite sure where it was going to lead.

I picked up the programs and placed them gingerly on the table. They seemed much heavier now. They were laden with relevance. They were the journeys of a theatrical group whose itinerary was so eccentric that it was obvious their art was diluted in the service of some other agenda. That agenda was the center on which the strands converged. I drank a third of a snifter of very elegant brandy. Bushy purred.

20

"Who?"

"Me, John. Alice . . . Alice Nestleton."

There was a silence on the other end of the phone. Poor John Cerise. I was obviously one of the few people he didn't want to hear from.

"John, don't worry. I'm not going to get you beat up again."

He laughed.

"Are your wounds healed?" I asked. I realized I should be ashamed of myself for not calling him before, when he got home from the hospital.

"I'm fine," he said, "just a bit stiff."

There was an awkward pause. Then he asked: "Did you ever find that white cat . . . Carla?"

"You mean Clara, John. Yes, she's alive and well and living in a pet shop."

"There's nothing like happy endings."

"Look, John, I need another favor from you," I said.

He laughed nervously.

"I want to borrow one of your cats . . . one of your Abyssinians."

"Borrow a cat? Why, Alice?"

"Well, it's really too complicated to explain, but it'll only be for a couple of days and I'll take good care of it."

"But I thought you told me your cats don't like visitors."

"Well, I won't keep the cat at my apartment—at a friend's."

"For how long, Alice?"

"A few days. It's just for some cat photographs for a friend of mine in advertising. He needs a beautiful Abyssinian and you have only beautiful Abyssinians." I was only half-lying to him. I did intend to take a photograph, but it was not really for advertising purposes. Or, rather, it was for a different kind of offering.

"Well, Alice, how can I get the cat to you?"

"My friend has a car. We'll pick the cat up tomorrow morning . . . about ten . . . will ten be okay?"

"Good. That will be good. Ten o'clock is fine. I'll let you have Jack Be Quick," he said.

I hung up the phone. God bless you, John Cerise, I thought. He could always be trusted. Risa was on the sofa, playing an elaborate kind of hide-and-seek with Bushy. I smiled at both of them. I felt wonderful. Ever since I discovered that the Nikolai Group was not what it had appeared to be—that it must have had a very secret agenda—the pieces had been falling into place. I had been to the library many times, burying myself in back issues of newspapers and journals. I had a full-scale model of past, present, and future— but it had to be proved, and the cat from John Cerise was the first step.

I walked, almost danced, to the window and stared down onto the street.

Madame Swoboda would be proud of me now, I thought. For wasn't that the essence of Method acting? One does not walk out onto a stage and begin to act. One walks out and speaks words or does motions and they are totally authentic because they come from authentic recollections and understanding of oneself. One doesn't act—one is. One doesn't fret in the wings, because there is nothing to fret about.

"Why are you so happy?" I heard Risa ask.

"Oh," I said, "just middle-age mirth."

"And where do you go all the time lately? You're never here."

"Research," I replied, "research, inquiry, analysis, a little here, a little there."

She cocked her head like a cat. She didn't know what I was talking about.

"I think, Risa, that I'm very close to finding out why Bruce Chessler died," I explained.

She stopped asking questions. She pulled into herself. I had forgotten how she must have loved him; I had never believed her attempt to distance herself from him.

About an hour later she seemed to revive. She said: "I think I'll move back to my apartment tomorrow. I don't want to interfere with your research, your analysis, your what-have-you."

Her voice was contemptuous. I didn't rise to the bait. I didn't want to argue with Risa about anything. Now she was furious for some reason, standing in the center of the room, her hands clenched on her waist. What kind of odd transference had she made to me?

"Research, analysis . . . why do you say such stupid things? What does it have to do with Bruce's murder? He's dead . . . he's off the planet . . . out of the universe . . . gone . . . dissipated . . . vanished. How can *you* find out why Bruce died? You didn't even know him!"

She spat her words out to me as if I were the mother who had betrayed her. Yes, it was time for the girl to go.

"Are you sure that cat is not going to jump around?" Basillio asked in a nervous voice. He kept staring through the rearview mirror at the beautiful Abyssinian cat pressed against the back seat of the car, his back arched.

"Don't worry, Tony, he loves it there, he won't bother you at all."

I was turned completely around, staring at the cat we had just picked up at John Cerise's. His name, I remembered, was Jack Be Quick. It was a very good name for a cat. He had a ruddy-brown coat ticked with black, and green eyes. He was lithe, hard, muscular, and gave off those signals in movement that seemed to say: "Yes, I not only look like a miniature cougar, I can act like one if you don't watch out." Of course, it was just a joke. Abyssinians are very kindly pussycats—exotic, yes, but kind. And Jack Be

Quick settled down very quickly, much to Tony's relief.

It wasn't until we were crossing the George Washington Bridge into Manhattan that Basillio said: "Swede, I really hope you know what you're doing this time."

"Are you frightened, Tony? It may well be the greatest performance of your life."

"Not frightened so much, Swede, as feeling stupid."

I patted his hand. "We all feel stupid sometimes, Tony," I said. "It can't be helped.

Basillio had been very difficult to convince this time. My plans were simple and straightforward. First I was going to create a bogus photograph of a white cat with black markings that looked very like Clara. And I was going to use the Abyssinian, Jack Be Quick, to accomplish that. Basillio said it could be done easily with color transparencies and all kinds of xerographic magic.

Then Basillio was going to take the photograph to Bukai and offer him the cat for ten thousand dollars. Bukai would throw him out. But then I knew a whole lot of interesting things were going to happen.

"And I think one of the reasons why I feel so stupid is that you refuse to tell me what you are doing," he complained.

I didn't reply. Why hadn't I confided in Basillio? I don't know. I usually did. But this crime seemed to be so elaborate, to consist of so many strands, to require the uncovering of so many details, that I simply had stopped using Basillio as an intellectual companion midway through. I really didn't know why. It dawned on me that his feelings must really be hurt—I had been ordering him around like he was a chauffeur . . . as if he worked for me. Maybe it had something to do with my meeting up once again with Joseph Grablewski. Yes, maybe that was it. I had heard that Grablewski had been discharged from the hospital. He was probably back in his Forty-fourth Street coffin once again, gazing down at his vodka.

When we finally pulled up in front of the copy shop, Jack Be Quick seemed to have developed a glaring affection for Basillio.

Once inside, Tony and an assistant got to work. I cannot really describe what happened. There were mounted Polaroid cameras . . . airbrushes . . . plastic overlays . . . strange whirrings and screechings . . . dripping pieces of material that seemed to come from a hospital laboratory.

But within two hours Basillio presented to me an 8½-by-11 photograph, or copy of a photograph, that was in dazzling color—a brilliant portrait of Jack Be Quick. Only Jack had changed colors.

He was now white with black spots on face and rump.

Magic. It was sheer magic. My hand began to tremble as I held it.

I had the delicious temptation to take a cab immediately to that pet store on Hudson Street where Clara and her two friends were incarcerated and then show it to Clara . . .

ask her opinion . . . ask her whether we had done a good job.

"Is that what you wanted?"

"Exactly," I replied.

"Well, they don't call Mother Courage the best full-service shop in downtown Manhattan for nothing," Basillio said. He winked at me. "Now what do we do?" he asked, staring at Jack Be Quick, who had leapt to the top of his desk and was staring longingly at his swivel chair.

"We proceed with the plan," I said.

"I was afraid you were going to say that."

It was just past two in the afternoon. Basillio and I stood across the street from Bukai's town house, making sure to be out of sight of the windows, more toward the Fifth Avenue end of the street.

Basillio was obviously nervous. It had been a long time since he'd played a difficult part.

"Okay, Swede," he said grimly, "let's go over this again. Step by step."

"Fine, Tony."

"Who am I?"

"No names. You're a guy who needs money. A lot of money fast. And you have what Bukai wants."

"You mean I have a white cat with black spots in my shop."

"Right."

"And I'll give it to him for ten thousand dollars."

"Right."

"And he has twenty-four hours to pay or forget it."

"Right."

"God, Swede, this is crazy. What kind of lunatic would pay ten thousand dollars for a white cat?"

"Just show him the photo, Tony. And tell the old man the cat is at Mother Courage. You'll deliver if he pays."

"Is he going to pay?"

"I don't think so, Tony. I'm banking that he won't."

"Then what's the point?"

"Are you ready, Tony?"

"Wait. What if I can't get in?"

"I told you. A young woman will answer the door. Tell her you want to see Bukai. Tell her Bruce Chessler sent you. You'll get in."

"I don't know why, Swede, but I find this very distasteful."

"I appreciate it, Tony."

He smiled. Then he drew his hand over his face as if he were changing masks, and what emerged was a snarling, ugly, yet strangely vulnerable thief . . . or gambler . . . or hustler.

"Look good?" he asked from the corner of his mouth.

"Right out of *The Threepenny Opera*," I assured him. Without another word he strode across the street to the doorway. I turned and started to walk toward the museum. It was there we would meet as soon as he finished his mission—by the small bar at the entrance of the museum cafeteria.

I didn't dawdle in the museum. I walked right to the appointed place and sat down on one of the divans and ordered a club soda with lime. The lunch crowd was gone but a group of German tourists were seated all around me.

Basillio arrived twenty-five minutes later. He knelt beside me as if he were imparting some kind of classified information.

"Okay, Swede. It was a piece of cake. I walked inside with the young woman. She pushed me into this room cluttered with books. Five minutes later this ancient Russian comes downstairs. I show him the photograph of Jack Be Quick turned white. I tell him I need ten thousand dollars fast. I'm in trouble, I tell him. The deal is simple, I tell him. Ten thousand right now in my hand. And I bring you the cat in a half-hour. Then I figure I'm going too fast. So I modify the offer. Five thousand down and five thousand when I bring the cat."

He paused and then stood up.

"What happened, Tony?"

He knelt again. "The old man just stares at me like he's looking at some kind of ghost or lunatic. Then he tells me to get out. That's all. He tells me to get out. I leave him the card in case he changes his mind. And I'm gone."

I leaned back and closed my eyes. The game, as they say, had begun. And the first serve I had called correctly.

"Anything else for the moment?" Basillio asked sardonically.

"No," I said, "but could you give me the key to the shop? I want to go over tonight and make sure Jack Be Quick is fed."

"How long are you going to keep the beast in my shop?" he asked.

"Not long, Tony, not long."

"Have to go," he said, slapped me very gently on the cheek as a sign of comradeship, and was gone.

I had to move quickly now, I realized—quickly and carefully.

Harry Hanks was seated at a desk that seemed to have been stolen from an insurance company—it was large and modern and the top was painted orange, which did not at all blend in with the green-and-white motif of the police precinct.

He was reading the *Daily News,* spread out on top of the desk as if he were hunting for coupons.

I stood in front of the desk for a long time before he even noticed me, and when he did, he didn't recognize me.

"May I sit down?" I asked, pointing to the empty chair next to the desk.

"What can I do for you, lady?"

I sat down and waited for him to fold up the paper and give me his undivided attention. He kept looking through the paper.

"Don't you remember me?"

"Not really," he said.

"We had a discussion in front of the Gramercy Park Hotel . . . about Bruce Chessler."

He grinned. He remembered. "Right, the lady who lost her student."

I didn't appreciate the sarcasm, but I really didn't have time to play games with him.

"Bruce Chessler was not murdered in a drug-related incident," I said to him.

He sat up suddenly, his eyes wide, folding the paper with disgust and shoving it across the desk.

"Say what, lady?"

"I said that Bruce Chessler was not murdered because of a drug deal gone bad, as you told me."

"Is that so?"

"Since the case has grown cold under your supervision," I reminded him, "I should think you'd be very happy at what I've told you.'

"I am happy, lady. I am so happy that I can't even move. Because if I move I'll fall down on the floor and roll over and out the window and they'll scrape me up still laughing, still happy."

There was a long silence. I had realized he was going to be difficult—but not this difficult. I dug into my purse and came out with the New York *Times* article about me, which stated how I had been commended by the Nassau County Police Department for resolving the Starobin murder. He read the article and handed it back to me.

"What do you want me to say, lady?"

"Nothing. Just take what I'm telling you seriously."

"What are you telling me?"

"That Bruce Chessler was not murdered because of drugs."

"Okay, lady. If you say so."

"And," I added, "I am very close to being able to present the entire conspiracy to you."

"What conspiracy?"

"It's a long story. It's a criminal conspiracy." Should I tell him that Arkavy Reynolds and Bruce Chessler were murdered by the same gun? No! I decided against even bringing up Arkavy's name. That would entail discussing Detective Felix . . . it would bring in other jurisdictions . . . other complexities. Cops are afraid of bureaucratic complexities. They are afraid their noses will be bitten off.

Hanks swept the *Daily News* off his desk onto the floor with an angry flourish. "And you have proof of this so-called conspiracy? Of course you have, lady. Right? And you know the names of his killers? Right, lady? That's why you're here busting my hump, because you know all these things that we dumb cops don't know. Right?"

I waited until his anger abated. He was a difficult man to deal with. Very difficult.

"I am going to say something to you that is very strange."

"Everything you told me or didn't tell me so far, lady, has been strange."

"There is a cat in a copy store only a few minutes from here."

"Is that so?"

"And within the next few hours someone is going to try to steal that cat."

"The excitement mounts."

"And the person who tries to steal that cat is the person who murdered Bruce Chessler."

"So you're going to be hiding there with your video camera, is that it? And you're going to sell the tape to Channel Seven news, and then you're going to write a book about the great criminal conspiracy . . . or was it the cat conpiracy?"

"You really dislike me, don't you, Detective?"

"You have it wrong, lady. I just don't like listening to fantasies."

I leaned over the desk and wrote the address on a small pad. He stared at what I had written.

"If you can spend the evening with me there, waiting, I will show you that they are not fantasies."

"Right, lady. After I get off work today, you want me to hold your hand for God knows how many hours in a copy shop, keeping our eyes on some cat."

"Yes, Detective Hanks. That is what I would like you to do."

"Well, lady, I have a better idea."

"What's that?"

He tore a sheet of paper off the same pad I had written on, wrote something on it, and pushed it at me.

"Now," he said, "I'm going to go home after work and take a shower and have a few drinks and then have some supper and then take a walk and maybe watch a ball game and then go to sleep. But if you're in that store staring at that cat and some killers come at you, well, you just tell them to hold on because you have to make a call—to me. That's my home number, lady."

The whole meeting had gone as wrong as it could go, from the very beginning. I realized it was to a large extent my fault. I shouldn't have expected Detective Harry Hanks to give me any help unless I gave him some very hard facts. I had dug up many of them, but it was too early to present them— to anyone. Perhaps Hanks would think them relevant. For me, they were pointers. No, it went much deeper than that. Hanks thought me a dilettante . . . it didn't matter how many newspaper clippings I showed him about my crime-solving prowess. And I thought Hanks to be an arrogant fool.

I took the piece of paper, crumpled it, and dropped it into my purse like a piece of dirty candy given to me by a derelict whose feelings I didn't want to hurt.

"You see," I said, "as difficult as this may seem to you, Detective Hanks, we are both after the same thing."

"Which is?"

"The person or persons who murdered Bruce Chessler."

"Fine. Call me if you need help," he said, and I saw he was making a strong effort to get rid of his sarcasm and skepticism . . . to be professional . . . to be noncommittal— while at the same time distancing himself from a woman he obviously found hard to deal with. He kept his body turned away from me as if he were desperate for me to leave but didn't want to say so . . . didn't dare to say so.

I stood up and started walking away.

"Wait," I heard him say.

I didn't turn back toward him; I just stopped.

"I forgot your name," he said.

"Alice Nestleton," I replied.

"Look, Miss Nestleton, you know I want that kid's killer. Just as much as you do."

"I suppose so."

"So you give me something solid and I'll move on it."

"That's what I'm about to do," I replied.

21

I had moved Basillio's swivel chair to the long hallway between the office and the shop. It was quiet and dark. A single light burned over one of the large copying machines and it spread diminishing rays throughout the hallway.

Jack Be Quick was nibbling some chicken I had bought him on the way over.

From time to time he stared slyly at me.

"They're coming to get you, Jack," I said. "Three old Russians are coming to rescue you because they think you're white with black spots."

Jack didn't seem to mind at all.

I leaned forward and watched him. How beautiful his breed was; how suffused with a sense of wildness and mystery; yes, it was true—the Abyssinian reeked of Egyptian deserts.

Then I sat back. I was tired but determined. I didn't know which of the three old men would be sneaking through the door. Maybe it would be all three. I didn't care. It wasn't revelation I was there for—it was confirmation. It would be the last piece in the puzzle and I could present it to the world. The world? I was thinking like an actress again, not a criminal investigator. It was humorous. The world didn't care about Bruce Chessler. And the world didn't really care about the strange, tortuous journey of those Russian émigrés, now sequestered in their hard-earned homes, thinking God knows what thoughts, being obsessed by geriatric memories.

Time went slowly. Very slowly. Again and again I walked to the two doors through which someone had to walk. The front door to the store and the side door, leading from the office to the alley.

Which door would it be? What did it matter? How would the break-in happen? What did it matter?

At midnight I pulled the swivel chair back into the office and pushed it behind the desk. I sat down and swiveled in the darkness.

Jack Be Quick leapt up on the desk. His green eyes gleamed. He circled the desk and made a very deep purring sound, from his belly. Was he still hungry? Did he want water? No, both were available to him.

"Speak to me, Jack," I said to him.

He approached me warily.

"A penny for your thoughts, Jack."

He stretched, his legs and large paws elongated downward; his back arched. Is there anything more beautiful than a handsome cat stretching in the shadows?

My thoughts went to Grablewski and then to Bruce Chessler. It was amazing how they always popped up together. And it was sad that my thoughts, when they focused on men, rarely dealt with past lovers . . . only with would-be lovers—men who were not . . . had never been . . . or could never be my lovers.

When I looked back up, Jack Be Quick had vanished from the desk. I could see his shadow against one of the walls.

I suddenly realized that I had nothing with me, no weapon in case of trouble. Nor did I have my bag or even a scarf. I had arrived at the Mother Courage Copying Shop like a Zen Buddhist monk, with only the clothes on my back. Why? I didn't really know. It was strange. Maybe I required simplicity in the face of a dense and grim conspiracy. Or maybe, since it had required a great deal of mental and physical effort to arrive at where I was in relation to the conspiracy—in relation to understanding how all the strands were proceeding toward an unfolding center—I had to be almost naked in my resolve.

The most horrible sound I have ever heard in my life suddenly cascaded through the store.

I didn't move. The sound seemed to splinter my bones . . . to make me shiver . . . to crush my will. I couldn't move.

Again and again . . . louder and louder . . .

It didn't stop. I closed my eyes. I scrunched down into the chair.

Glass. It sounded like glass shattering. Someone was smashing in the front window of the store.

I covered my ears. I got up. I pressed my

hands tight against my ears until they hurt. I ran into the hallway and then toward the front of the store. I didn't know what I was doing. I didn't know what was happening.

I let my hands drop from my ears. The sound began again . . . splintering, screeching, moaning, lunacy.

I could see something now.

Someone was smashing in the front window.

I started to scream.

The figure was inside now, through the window.

I looked around, desperate, searching for something to stop the intruder.

And then there was absolute silence. It was so quiet that I could hear the pads of Jack Be Quick's feet.

The intruder heard them also—the intruder was there for the white cat that did not exist.

Where was the light? I thought desperately. There must be a switch on the wall. Where *was* the light? I ran my hand along the wall like a crazed blind person. My hand touched something. I pushed up. The whole store was flooded with light.

In front of me, holding a steel pipe, stood a small thin black woman with a closely shaved head.

My God, it was the poet! It was the young woman from the bar! It was Elizabeth.

She stared at me. Exhausted. Frightened. Panting.

She dropped the iron bar that had splintered the window. It clattered to the floor. There were streaks of blood on her wrists.

"Why are you here?" she asked in a hoarse whisper, terrified.

"To make sure you don't get the white cat," I said.

I ran back and gathered Jack Be Quick in my arms and approached her, thrusting the large nonwhite Abyssinian close to her face.

"You see, there is no white cat here, none at all. We were just waiting for you."

Her eyes roamed over the walls and the windows and the machines, as if she were searching for a way out.

"Who sent you?" I asked.

She seemed to draw inside of herself.

"Was it Bukai . . . or Chederov . . . or Mallinova?"

She shook her head. "I don't know those names."

"Then who?"

"I don't know his name."

"He paid you?"

"No. He didn't pay. He paid for what happened in the bar. He paid me to point out Bruce. And then he threatened me. He said if I broke in here and got the white cat, he'd forget everything. If not, he'd tell the police that I was an accessory to murder."

"Why did you point him out?"

"I didn't know he would be murdered. I had no idea. I just wanted some extra money. Some spending money. You know—for books and things. Don't you believe me? I had no idea."

Her legs gave way. She sprawled on the floor. I remembered our conversation in the bar, about that Indian philosopher—Pantajali.

"How much did he pay you to point him out?"

"Five hundred dollars."

"And what else did he get for the money?"

"Nothing, I swear. Just that I would hold the booth in the bar so that Bruce would be there; so that he would not see the bar was too crowded and go elsewhere. That was all I had to do. Talk with Bruce in a booth until he came in."

"Who is he?"

"I told you, I don't know his name."

She started to weep. She kept raising her hands as if to explain, and then lowering them.

"Did you have a phone number?" I asked.

"Yes."

"Give it to me."

She shook her head. She was clearly frightened.

"Give it to me," I said, closing in on her.

She stared at me as if evaluating what kind of threat I represented, as if determining how far I was prepared to go. She understood she was in very deep hot water . . . either with the police or with the man who had hired her in the beginning.

Then she removed a crumpled paper from her pocket.

A phone number was penciled on one side.

I dialled the number. A recorded message came on. The voice said: "You have reached

Sedaka & Son, Diamond Merchants. If you are using a pushbutton phone, please press One for our accounting department . . . press Two to schedule an appointment . . . press Three if your call is personal. Thank you.'' The phone fell gently out of my hand and back on the receiver.

I smiled grimly. Everything was going just fine. Jack Be Quick walked regally over to the squatting, frightened poet and rubbed his back against her knee. She seemed to shrink further into herself.

22

I was sitting next to Detective Harry Hanks in his ugly unmarked police car, holding Jack Be Quick on my lap. We were double-parked across from the Café Vivaldi.

It had not been easy getting him there. The scene in the police precinct had been volatile.

"So what do you want me to do? Arrest the girl for breaking your friend's plate-glass window? Okay. I'll do that. Or do you want me to arrest her for attempted kidnapping of a white cat that didn't turn out to be a white cat at all?" He was getting more and more irritated and he started accentuating his questions by poking his finger in the air. "Or do you want me to arrest her for accessory to murder? That's it, isn't it? That the same guy who paid her to steal the cat and to set up Bruce Chessler also murdered Bruce Chessler."

"Calm down, Detective."

"No, you calm down, lady. Because that little black girl never saw a person she could identify in the bar that night. She was there when the shots were fired, but she didn't know who fired them. Were you ever in that bar, lady? Of course you were. Where the kid was sitting, you can't see your hand in front of your face. So you want me to arrest the black girl and the diamond merchant on the basis of phone calls? You must be kidding."

"I have a lot more," I told him.

"Where? In your pocketbook? In your shoes?"

"No, in a café not far from here."

And that was how, after a struggle, we ended up in the unmarked police car, staring across the street, against a strong sun, into a coffeehouse.

"These three old Russians . . . how do you know they're inside now? I can't see a thing."

"Oh, they're in there," I said. "The owner of the café told me. They have met for years on the last Thursday of each month."

"Listen, lady," he said, exasperated, "I don't want any more conflict with you. Just tell me what you want me to do and I'll do it. Then just promise to leave me alone."

"Go in with me, Detective, and protect me when I confront them," I said.

"From what you told me about their ages . . . are you sure they're assaultive?" he asked.

"We'll see, won't we?"

"Do we really need the cat?"

"Oh, yes, we really do," I replied.

We left the car double-parked. We shut the doors. The three of us, including Jack Be Quick, walked through the door of the Café Vivaldi.

The three old men were sitting at the same table I had seen them sitting at before—that time I had followed Bukai to the pet store on Hudson Street where he had sequestered the white cats.

For a moment I was frightened . . . very frightened . . . not physically . . . and I clutched poor Jack Be Quick so tightly in my arms that he gave a long low growl.

That was when the three turned toward me. I had never been this close to Chederov and Mallinova. Chederov had thick white hair that fell down over the most lined face I had ever seen. Mallinova had a painfully thin lantern face. They were all wearing cramped suits, as if they were the board of directors of some long-closed bank.

"May I join you, Mr. Bukai? We've already met, if you remember. And this is my friend Detective Harry Hanks." At the mention of the detective, they stared at each other. They said nothing. Detective Hanks pulled two chairs up to the large round table. We sat down. I still held Jack Be Quick.

There was a double glass of espresso in front of each of the old men. And toward the center of the table were two untouched pieces of Italian cheesecake.

No one spoke for what seemed the longest time. I could hear Bukai breathing heavily to my left.

It was I who must talk. But to whom? It was I who was going to indict them. But who was going to receive the indictment? It had to be the detective. I would talk to Harry Hanks.

I was about to do the kind of theater piece

I had always despised: a one-woman monologue reciting facts. But there was no other option.

I began. Detective Hanks was the audience. I ignored the other three.

"We are sitting with three rich old men. They came to America penniless except for their reputations as dramatic artists, as professionals in the world's most prestigious theater company—the Moscow Art Theater.

"Now they are very wealthy men. How did they get their money?

"Let me tell you. They formed a theater group in the 1950s—the Nikolai Group—and it survived for ten years.

"Each year the Group made a trip to South and Central America to perform.

"I have traced the itinerary of that group. It is very odd. One oddity is that they visited only countries or cities that were in the midst of either political or economic turmoil. Isn't that strange? One would think they would avoid those places. Most theatrical companies do. But not the Nikolai Group. Oh, no."

I hesitated and looked around the table. Mallinova was very pale. Bukai was grimacing and stirring his espresso with a tiny silver spoon.

"You see," I continued, "they weren't on tour for aesthetic reasons. They were smuggling in diamonds and smuggling out cash. For diamonds have traditionally been the repository of wealth for South Americans during wars and revolutions and inflation. In

France and the Middle East, it is gold. But in South America it is diamonds."

Hanks arched his eyebrows. I slid across the table to him a piece of paper I had prepared; on one side was the Group's itinerary in South America . . . on the other side the visits were correlated with social, economic, or political turmoil. Hanks studied the sheet.

"It's a helluva coincidence," he noted. He pushed the paper toward the center of the table for any of the old men to study. None of them made a move toward the paper.

"But it's circumstantial as hell," he added.

I continued. I was beginning to grow into the heady role. I felt a sense of analytical power . . . that I was projecting it.

"We all know that Mr. Bukai is a partner in a diamond firm now run by a gentleman named Sedaka. His father, Daniel Sedaka, died in 1972. He died at home, among his family, content. But if you will retrieve from your files, Detective Hanks, a May 11, 1949, article in a now-defunct newspaper called the *Daily Mirror*, it describes how three individuals were indicted for the theft of a large shipment of diamonds consigned from Amsterdam to New York. One of those individuals was Daniel Sedaka. The diamonds vanished in Toronto. The senior Mr. Sedaka was tried but the jury refused to convict. Those diamonds were eventually sold on the black market in South America for huge sums of cash. And it was all clear profit."

Mallinova raised his hand for the waiter

and gestured that he wanted water. I waited until the water was served.

"So," I continued, "the Nikolai Group eventually disbanded, with everyone happy—everyone rich. But then, alas, a crazy young man comes on the scene. He is the grandson of a colleague—Maria Swoboda. I'm talking about Bruce Chessler."

Mallinova drank his water. I could see his eyes staring through the top of his glass at Bukai.

"Now, Bruce Chessler was a very tormented young man. He lived a marginal existence . . . a typically pathetic out-of-work actor's life, surviving through small-time drug sales. One of his customers was a theater hanger-on named Arkavy Reynolds. One day, probably, Arkavy needed speed and had no money, so he gave Bruce Chessler some information instead. Dirty information . . . about some revered people. Arkavy thought Bruce would find their diamond-smuggling scheme amusing. How Arkavy got the information, we'll never know. But he was a very resourceful lunatic. Anyway, Bruce didn't find it amusing. Bruce loved the theater with a passion and he hated those who debased it. The hypocrisy of his grandmother's colleagues—these hallowed names from the Moscow Art Theater—began to fester in him. Since they were thieves, he reasoned, he would steal something from them.

"Bruce Chessler didn't steal money from them. He stole something much more prized by the old Russians—their last link to the

Stanislavski tradition of the Moscow Art Theater. You see, Stanislavski had a white cat named Constantin, with black spots on face and rump. And soon there were kittens and many such cats. And when the émigrés left Russia, they took their felines with them, and once in this country, they kept the line alive. If you want to see them, Detective Hanks, we can go to a pet store on Hudson Street, where they are now being boarded. There are three white cats with black spots in there. They belong to these old gentlemen here, and they were what Bruce Chessler stole.

"What a stupid childish act it was . . . stealing cats from old people. And then he just gave them away. He gave them away because he intuited that he had gone too far . . . that the three old men were afraid he was going to go to the police about the diamond smuggling of so many years ago. It never dawned on the old men that Bruce Chessler had absolutely no hard evidence and that the statute of limitations made any prosecution improbable. What they really wanted to protect above all were their reputations . . . their delusions that they were artists . . . that the great Moscow Art Theater tradition rested nobly on their brows. So our three elderly friends had to make sure. They had to get rid of that irrational, vindictive young man. After all, he was threatening their immortality. They acted murderously. They frightened Sedaka Junior into killing Bruce Chessler and his bohemian information source, Arkavy Reynolds, and then stealing back the cats.

"You see, the Russians were not merely silent partners in the diamond firm. They owned the controlling interest. If Sedaka refused to comply with their wishes, they could have simply fired him. And Sedaka lived a very expensive lifestyle. He chose to murder rather than be poor. I'm sure, Detective Hanks, that if you put a little pressure on the diamond merchant, he will happily implicate his benefactors to cut his own sentence."

I leaned back, suddenly exhausted, talked out. My throat was beginning to tremble.

Detective Hanks was staring at me, obviously absorbed in my story.

I turned to Bukai. He, too, was staring at me. I smiled at him.

He picked up his espresso glass and flung the contents into my face. It happened so fast I couldn't evade the lukewarm coffee which splattered over me.

Hanks stood up swiftly and started toward the old man. I raised my hand to stop him. He sat back down, reluctantly.

I wiped the coffee away, carefully, with Bukai's napkin, and then wiped Jack Be Quick's face, since he also had been splattered.

"Yes," I said, "these old men love their white cats so much they will go to great lengths to get them back if stolen. They were even going to take Jack Be Quick, whose photograph I had doctored to simulate a white cat with black spots. Why? Because they thought Bruce Chessler had stolen it from another émigré. They were the guardians of the white cats . . . as if that would redeem their prostitution. Stupid, sad old men, willing to do anything to die with some semblance of honor.''

I stood up and placed Jack Be Quick on the center of the table.

"Now, there's a reason why I could use Jack Be Quick as a stand-in for one of the white cats. The white cats bear an uncanny physical resemblance to Abyssinians—which Jack Be Quick is. But they're not Abyssinians at all . . . they're just plain old Moscow Art Theater wardrobe cats.''

I pushed Jack Be Quick gently onto his back and began to stroke his stomach. He lay there happily.

"Look at him, Detective Hanks,'' I said.

"I'm looking. So what?''

"Can you see what makes Abyssinians different from other cats . . . why they look like cougars?''

"The paws . . . they're bigger.''

"No, the pads, not the paws. They have larger pads on the feet.''

"Okay, okay, so what?''

"Well, Detective, why don't you just take a peek into Jack Be Quick's front-left paw?''

"Why?''

"He has an important present for you.''

He reached over, gently spread the pad, and said: "There's something in there.''

"Right.'' I reached over and pulled out a small diamondlike stone.

"Is this the way they smuggled the diamonds? I know South American animal quarantine laws are a joke, but . . ."

I laughed. Tweaking the detective's nose was refreshing. But enough was enough.

"I have no idea how they smuggled the diamonds in and the cash out, Detective. Probably in their underwear. But in those years, before the drugged-out rock bands, traveling theatrical groups were never searched by customs agents in any country. It was a long-honored gentleman's agreement. In the 1950s, for example, a well-known British ballerina visited this country often with her troupe and her constant companion—a bottle of Polish vodka . . . which was illegal to bring into the country at that time. No one bothered her. In those days, before the rock bands forced them to crack down, artists traveling on tour could bring into a given country whatever they wanted—and take out what they wanted. Provided they were discreet."

I dropped the fake stone, actually a pebble, into Bukai's empty espresso cup. Jack Be Quick walked over to inspect what he had been carrying.

The waiter dropped the bill onto the table. It was such an absurd ending to my performance that I started to laugh. Then I looked around. No one else was laughing. The faces of the three men had crumbled. Their bodies seemed to have been scraped of substance.

I turned away from them, toward the door to the café, and stared for a long time. I had the strangest feeling that Bruce Chessler was about to walk in. What a bizarre delusion. Did

I require applause from his ghost? For what? For a fine performance? For unraveling the conspiracy? For making sure that the old men would probably die in a penitentiary somewhere rather than in their town houses? It was hard to understand.

23

"It's not often a beautiful woman buys me lunch in a restaurant where the house salad costs twenty-two-fifty," Basillio said, staring at his sparsely laden plate with both horror and awe.

We were seated in one of those posh new restaurants on lower Broadway, south of Houston and north of Canal.

A week had gone by. I felt very good. I was still celebrating. Sedaka had blown the whistle on the three old men. Hanks said he'd get twenty years to life for the Chessler and Reynolds murders. As for the three old men, Hanks had no idea what they'd get. How does one sentence eighty-five-year-old men? I wasn't celebrating their coming pain; I was celebrating the truth, which was, in an odd sense, a vindication of Stanislavski and the Moscow Art Theater. I don't know how, but it was. It was as if the Russian theatrical tradition had hired me and paid me with unspoken affection.

"What I still don't understand, Swede, is how you tied together the fact that there was something strange about the Nikolai Group's tours and the fact they only went to countries where diamonds would be very much in demand because of turmoil."

"Well, look Tony, I've been around the theater too long not to recognize that those tours were somehow fakes. Theater companies can't do it that way. The Group had to be going to each specific country for a reason, and that reason had to be lucrative. What little underfunded company can fly down to Rio for two days with their whole cast and baggage and then turn around and fly back? No way. So I took the month, year, and place of each trip and checked it against the New York Times Index for those dates. Each visit was the same—the Nikolai Group seemed to be courting danger. They went only to places that were in turmoil one way or another. They had to be bringing something in or bringing something out. Then I remembered that Bukai's original connection with the diamond firm had been with the father, not the son. So I started researching old man Sedaka . . ."

"And the rest is history," Basillio added, grinning.

"The white cats are still a problem," I said, suddenly noticing one of the strangest little rolls I have ever seen nestled in the wicker bread tray. I extracted it and studied it as a cat would.

"Where are they?"

"Oh, they're still in the pet store. But the pet-store owner won't release them unless Bukai signs a consent order. And the old man won't sign anything. He wants them to stay there. He still believes other white cats exist and are being threatened."

"What about the fake white cat?"

"You mean Jack Be Quick? He's back with his owner."

"I still don't understand why they tried to steal him."

"Bukai and his friends obviously lost count of the progeny of Constantin. They don't know which émigrés own which cats. That's why he went for Jack Be Quick. He didn't know if it really was a descendant of Constantin's. It sure looked like one. Better sure than sorry."

"Only in the theater," he mused, finally giving up on the salad and staring at the remarkable dessert wagon that hovered in the distance.

I realized that I was still holding the strange roll, so I dropped it back into the basket.

"Eat it, Swede, it's good for you. It'll fatten you up."

"I like bread in the morning only."

"You always were weird, Swede," he said. I thanked him profusely for his compliment. We sat there for another half-hour or so, eating tarts and drinking delicious coffee. Then he went back to work and I started home.

On Fourth Avenue, just before Fourteenth Street, I passed a flower store and saw an expensive bouquet of yellow flowers. I bought it and kept walking.

When I reached Twenty-third Street I stopped. I was perplexed. Why was I going home? The cats were fed. There was nothing more to do. Why had I bought the flowers? For *him?*

I stepped into the gutter and hailed a cab, which took me to Forty-fourth Street. Had I really bought the flowers for Joseph Grablewski in celebration that he was out of the alkie ward in the hospital? But he had been out a while.

I walked gingerly into the bar. I was excited, like a girl on a date.

He was there, in the same booth. I started to walk toward him, self-conscious, like at an audition. My vulnerability angered me. God, I was past forty. I had never even slept with that drunkard.

I slipped into the booth across from him and laid the flowers on the table. A glass of what looked like cola was in front of him.

"Another attempt at seduction?" he asked weakly, staring at the flowers.

He looked pale and thin and his hair was cut shorter. He kept his hands palm-down on the table. They were shaking slightly.

"How do you feel?"

"Wonderful."

"Where's your vodka?"

"Don't you know . . . I'm now a recovering alcoholic."

"What's in the glass?"

"Root beer."

"I want to thank you for your help . . . for the information you gave me."

"What help?" he asked.

"About Lev Bukai's diamond connections."

"Were you one of the people who visited me in the hospital?"

"Yes."

Since he hadn't even seemed to remember anything about Lev Bukai, I left it alone.

"Why?"

"Why what?"

"Why did you visit me in the hospital?"

"To bring you flowers," I said, smiling and pointing to them.

"I don't like flowers . . . in hospitals . . . in bars . . . onstage."

I pulled the flowers close to me.

"What do we do? What do we do? Sleep together or not?" He recited the questions in a singsong manner and then began to laugh.

"You must forgive me," he finally said. "Sobriety brings out my lack of control. But it won't last long. I've never been able to achieve sobriety for more than three days running."

"Maybe this time."

"That's what my students always say."

I was perplexed. What students was he talking about?

"Do you teach now?"

"When sober. Didn't you know? Don't you know that for the past ten years the great Joseph Grablewski has been earning vodka money by teaching psychotic students how to really act . . . how to bring heaven, hell, Marx, and De Sade into their genitalia."

"No, I had no idea you were an acting coach."

"Coach? My God! Not a coach. Never a

coach. Master, guru, savior, shrink—but not ever a coach."

He drank some of the root beer, very slowly, as if it could kill him.

"Everybody's heard of crazy Joseph Grablewski's classes."

"I haven't. Who studies with you? Maybe I know some of them."

"Psychopaths study with me," he yelled, "and those who are heartbroken and those who despise what there is, and those who are broken by the stage, and those who . . . Not you, lady, never a beautiful lady like you."

He had misjudged me again. He had made me into the enemy again.

"I don't make them feel good. I don't prepare them for stupid plays. I make them into performance artists. I make them grapple with the world. Sometimes it even kills them."

"You're talking stupid now, Joseph. Calm down."

"Am I talking stupid? Am I really? What do you know? A student of mine was murdered a few weeks ago. What an actor he might have become under my tutelage! His assignment was simple: I told him to fall desperately in love with a woman . . . to pine for her . . . to write her love letters . . . to engage her . . . to go to the very limits of romantic fakery . . ."

I put my hands over my ears. I suddenly understood what I was hearing. But I could not deal with the horror of what I was comprehending. I wanted to be dumb, to be senseless.

Grablewski was still talking. I could see his lips moving wildly.

I ran out, spilling the flowers onto the floor. Bruce Chessler had loved me as an assignment! As a classroom exercise projected out onto the world! I walked ten, fifteen, twenty blocks, quickly. Then I stopped, exhausted. And right there, on the street, I began to laugh. Had ever an actress been so elegantly hoisted on her own petard?

24

Thanksgiving came and went. Christmas came and went. In January the diamond merchant Sedaka was sentenced to twenty-five years to life for the murder of Bruce Chessler. The charges against him for the murder of Arkavy Reynolds were dropped. The three old émigrés were sentenced to eight to fifteen years each for conspiracy to murder. All charges relating to diamond smuggling and theft were dropped. Mallinova died from a heart attack two weeks after the sentencing. Chederov suffered a stroke and was hospitalized. Only Bukai, of the three, went to jail.

I don't like to see people sent to the penitentiary, but I really had no sympathy for the Russians and Sedaka. They were murderers. In fact, I was on a sort of permanent high because it had been my efforts that solved the case. As for Joseph Grablewski's revelation that the young man's love for me was an acting-class exercise—well, I felt a bit stupid, but then I realized that it was probably my swallowing the tale of "doomed love" that had started my investigations. So my foolishness had paid off.

Everything was going well with me. There was a good possibility that I would land the part of an old crazy woman in a very strange and very beautiful play written by a Chilean woman, which was to be staged in the spring at Princeton University by a new drama society. I loved playing old crazy women with thick corrosive makeup dripping all over. It was a harmless perversion. As for cat-sitting, it was always there when I needed it.

My own cats were doing quite well, although Pancho had developed a mange-type rash on his back that required me to rub some evil-smelling substance on it a few times a week. This meant I had to catch Pancho. Which in turn meant that I was becoming physically fit, because to catch Pancho when he knew he was about to get anointed was more than difficult. I had to plot strategies . . . to lie in wait for him and then pounce. Once I grabbed him, he would fix his betrayed eyes on me until the deed was done. Poor Pancho, he never really trusted me.

In fact, I was so "up," I decided to buy a toaster-oven. It was just when I was percolating in the last phase of that decision that Basillio called and asked me to meet him for a drink.

The moment I saw him at the bar on Second Avenue just north of St. Marks Place, I knew he had something important to tell me; a plum of some kind. He was drumming a tune on the bar and bouncing up and down.

He patted the stool next to him. I sat.

"Now," he said grandly, "before I begin

telling you my news, I have to ask you a personal question."

"How personal?" I asked, ordering a glass of club soda with a twist.

"Trust me, Swede, trust me. What I want to know is: have you gotten over Joseph Grablewski?"

I exploded. "What are you talking about? Nothing happened between him and me. Nothing. It was just a kind of nostalgia for me. You were the one who sent me to him. Remember? Yes, I was happy to see him again, and acted like a little girl. But nothing happened. Nothing could happen. He's a walking tragedy. I haven't seen him in months. It was another one of my temporary aberrations."

"Good. I was afraid that if I gave you some terrific news about him, it might send you into a tailspin. You did love him once, Swede."

I sipped the club soda. He was insulting me, in a way. He was saying I would begrudge Joseph Grablewski some kind of happiness. He was saying I was a vindictive spurned woman.

All I said was: "Tony, you're very close to getting some club soda on your head."

He laughed, kissed me on the head, and pulled a newspaper clipping out of his pocket. Dramatically, with flourishes, he spread it out in front of me.

It was an advertisement from the theater section of the *Village Voice*:

ANNOUNCING THE WORLD PREMIERE OF . . .
Why Not?
By the famous Russian Symbolist Poet
A. A. Blok
Produced and directed by
Joseph Grablewski
The long-lost play by the most respected artist of revolutionary Russia is finally brought to the stage, in English, directed by one of the legends of the American theater.

The advertisement then went on to announce that the first previews would be the week of February 19 at the Cherry Lane Theater. Then it listed the cast and some other credits.

I sat back, astonished. It was truly wonderful. Almost wondrous. The man seemed to have risen from the dead. I remembered the last time I'd seen him, in the bar, when he had said his usual limit for sobriety was three days.

I turned to Basillio. I was crying. I said to him: "Believe me, Tony, I am extremely happy for him."

He nodded in assent. I could see that he too was engaged with the sheer heroism or luck or whatever it was that had prompted the reemergence of Joseph Grablewski.

But all he said was: "I never knew he wrote a play."

"Who?"

"Blok. I read all his poems as a kid. Remember *The Twelve?*"

I had heard of that long revolutionary poem, but I had never read it.

"I think Blok died in 1921." Basillio kept talking about Blok, slowly at first, and then escalating into one of his crazed drama lectures about the problems of putting poets on in the theater . . . about how you needed plain speech.

I wasn't listening. I wanted to do something. I wanted to celebrate. I wanted to give Joseph Grablewski something . . . a poem . . . a flower. I wanted to let him know that everyone who ever listened to him in the old days, everyone who ever heard him talk about theater, was grateful.

"Remember what he looked like when we visited him in the hospital?" Basillio suddenly asked.

Then it dawned on me what I must give him. I had in my possession what he really would appreciate—the love letters his pupil had penned to me as an exercise. Yes, Bruce Chessler's letters.

"Have to go, have to go," I called out as I started out of the bar.

"Wait, Swede, wait . . . where the hell are you going?"

But I was gone. I was walking back to my apartment, fast. I was like a twelve-year-old kid who has finally found the right gift for her teacher.

Sixty seconds after I flew through the front door of my apartment, scaring poor Bushy half to death, my enthusiasm dampened.

I couldn't find the letters where I thought I had left them.

I couldn't find them in the cartons. I

couldn't find them in the closets . . . or the files . . . or the cabinets . . . or the valises. They were nowhere . . . gone . . . vanished.

My balloon was deflated. But where were they?

Risa! It had to be Risa! She probably took them with her when she left.

How sad! It was probably her pathetic way of getting back at me. She probably also thought that Chessler's love for me was legitimate—not a classroom exercise. She didn't know it was all a fake.

It was stupid . . . sad . . . I wanted the letters back . . . I wanted to give them to Joseph. I started searching for Risa's phone number, remembering that I had written it down on a piece of paper after she had put it on my wrist with a Magic Marker. I found it and dialed. A voice answered. It wasn't Risa. The voice said there was no such person as Risa living there and never had been.

I hung up the phone. Could Risa have given me the wrong number by mistake? Unlikely. Could I have transcribed the wrong number from my wrist to the pad? Never. If there is one iron law of life, it is this: actors and actresses never make mistakes in phone numbers. They can't! Phone numbers are crucial. Directors, producers, agents, jobs, hairdressers. I have done a lot of wrong things in my life but I never dialed a number that I had transcribed wrong. My head is like a desktop computer when it comes to phone numbers.

Maybe Risa was not in fact Risa. Then who was she? And where did she live? The astonishing fact was that I had never even found out the girl's last name when she was staying in my apartment.

If she was, however, not who she said she was—then what really was her relationship to Bruce Chessler?

And if she was, in fact, Bruce Chessler's lover, then she had to know that the love letters were fake—an acting assignment. Lovers in the theater discuss acting classes.

Therefore, if she knew the love letters were fake, why would she want to steal them from my apartment?

Was there something in the letters I had missed? Some kind of code? To what end? Coding what?

I dressed warmly and walked to the New School, where I had taught the summer before. There was something there I had to see and had neglected to pick up. It was the bunch of short essays I had asked my students to write on that first day of class. The subject matter was "Theater," and all I wanted from them was a kind of ad hoc free association to that word.

The New School had sent me several postcards to pick up the papers and other pieces of property I had left behind after the summer term was over—a small umbrella and a few books.

I found them in a massive file hidden behind boxes in the old faculty lounge, categorized under N—for Nestleton.

I leafed through the papers quickly. Few were more than one page in length. It had turned out to be an idiotic exercise, but what did that matter? I wasn't interested in literary enlightenment or psychological truths.

I found Bruce Chessler's one-page effort.

What I had suspected or feared turned out to be absolutely true.

The paper I was holding in my hand and the love letters that Risa had stolen from my closet were not written by the same person.

Had Risa written the letters for Bruce? If so, so what? Lots of girlfriends help their boyfriends out in acting classes.

It didn't make sense, her stealing the letters, when she had written them.

I walked out of the New School, dropping the entire file in the garbage. It was freezing cold outside, but I walked slowly . . . very slowly. What else about little Risa was fake? Maybe her red punk hair? What about the murderous attack that drove her from her apartment to mine? Was that a lie? Why not? Was the point of that to be able to steal the love letters?

I started walking downtown, toward the Cherry Lane Theater, where Joseph Grablewski would be rehearsing.

Across the street from the theater was a building awning that shielded an outside alcove from the wind. I nestled in the alcove, keeping my eyes glued to the stage door. The cold meant nothing to me. This new thread, Risa, was fascinating.

It began to grow dark. The rehearsal was over. Couples and solitary individuals began to exit, their shoulders bent against the wind as they walked off.

I felt like I was in an old Katherine Hepburn movie, waiting in the darkness outside a Broadway theater . . . a kind of *Stage Door* adventure . . . Stage Door Alice Nestleton. I felt an intellectual apprehension that was so palpable it seemed to smell, like my brain was churning, smoking . . . an absurd imagery.

Then Joseph walked out. He was dressed for a summer day. His only tribute to winter was a beat-up scarf wrapped like a European talisman around his neck.

He leaned against the theater, waiting.

I knew what he was waiting for. He was staring across the street, but he didn't see me. Why would he notice? I was not on his mind.

Time passed. We were frozen in our places. Was it a half-hour? An hour? I didn't know.

A young woman appeared on the uptown corner. She started to walk slowly toward the theater.

As she got closer, she began to walk fast, then run.

She flung herself into Joseph's waiting arms. They embraced wildly. Their passion for each other seemed to radiate and make me weak. She began to kiss him, crazily, holding his head between her hands.

I stared at the old alcoholic and the young woman I knew as Risa.

I knew then that even though the murderers of Bruce Chessler were safely in prison or dead, there was another scenario that could explain the murder.

It was a very possible scenario.

It was very clear to me.

Risa had listened as Bruce spewed out his hatred for the émigrés . . . for their hypocrisy . . . for their diamond smuggling.

She helped him steal the white cats as a vindictive lark . . . as a bizarre way to pay them back for their betrayal of the Moscow Art Theater.

She wrote the love letters he needed for his acting-class assignment with Joseph Grablewski.

Then something unforseen happened.

She fell in love with Joseph Grablewski.

She wrote blackmail letters to Bukai and his associates, threatening them with disclosure of their diamond smuggling.

The émigrés believed it was Bruce Chessler who was blackmailing Bukai.

At first they paid up, not knowing who was collecting the payoff.

But then the demands became too steep. So they murdered Chessler, never knowing that Risa was the blackmailer.

And what were Risa's demands?

Money, of course, money. They had plenty.

But something else, also—some of the many valuable scripts the émigrés had managed to smuggle out of Russia when they fled. Among them A. A. Blok's *Why Not?*

Which scenario was correct? I didn't know.

Risa and Grablewski started to walk. Their

arms were locked almost desperately. I watched them until they vanished from sight.

Suddenly I was cold. I started home. As I walked, I began to think about Clara. I hoped she was in a good home—a home with a samovar.

1

Why was the woman whispering?

I had been in the Salzmans' apartment for about twenty minutes when I finally realized that Mrs. Salzman had whispered to me from the moment I entered. And that I had whispered back. The entire conversation was being conducted in whispers.

I was there to be interviewed for a cat-sitting job. Mrs. Salzman needed someone to visit her lonely feline three mornings a week while she was seeking medical treatment in a neighboring state. In other words, she would be sleeping elsewhere and her cat had to be reassured. The nature of the medical treatment was never mentioned, nor were the whereabouts of Mr. Salzman, if, indeed, he existed at all.

The cat's name was Abelard.

When the cat's name was revealed to me, I had a sudden insight that Mrs. Salzman was quite mad . . . that her cat had been surgically altered and the poor woman was caught in a delusion that her cat had been altered for love of Heloise. She was acting out a medieval castration romance. But the thought vanished as quickly as it had emerged; it was only one of my dramaturgical fantasies—an occupational hazard for actresses.

Mrs. Salzman kept whispering to me what a lovely cat he was.

The problem was—where was he? I couldn't see him.

"He's very frightened of people," Mrs. Salzman said, which was the first rational reason she had presented for the whispering.

Mrs. Salzman lived in a very confused apartment on East 37th Street in Manhattan. The furniture, and there was a lot of it, lined the walls like a military procession. Abelard could be under any of the pieces.

If I couldn't see Abelard, maybe I could hear him. Maybe I could hear his movements. Maybe that was another reason she kept whispering . . . so as to be aware of Abelard's movements.

"I am so happy to be able to deliver Abelard to a real professional cat sitter," Mrs. Salzman whispered.

I burst out laughing, very loudly. I couldn't help myself. Mrs. Salzman drew back, shocked, her hand involuntarily smoothing her hair. She was an impeccably dressed woman except for garish green leather shoes.

It was impossible to explain to her why her remark had collapsed me into laughter. But only two hours before I had entered Mrs. Salzman's Murray Hill apartment, I had been reading a short squib about myself in the neighborhood newspaper *Our Town.* The anonymous *"People"* columnist had mentioned me as a neighborhood resident and had noted: "The stately, long-haired, still-beautiful Alice Nestleton is one of our finest little-known actresses . . . little-known because of her penchant for obscure roles in obscure off-off-off Broadway plays."

The anonymous columnist then went on to add: "Alice Nestleton has long been a cult heroine to theater buffs."

The comment was absurd. Where were these "buffs"? In the supermarket on Third Avenue? I never met them.

Anyway, the whole point about that ludicrous description of me in the newspaper was that it *didn't* make me laugh. But it laid the groundwork. And when Mrs. Salzman characterized me two hours later as a "real professional cat sitter," the cumulative effect made me laugh out loud, heartily, raucously.

Mrs. Salzman quickly forgave my outburst and took me on a brief tour of her convoluted apartment. She pointed out the location of the cat food and the watering can for the plants and the lists of emergency numbers and several other key locations and objects.

There was still no sign of Abelard.

"What kind of cat is Abelard?" I asked.

"A lovely cat," replied Mrs. Salzman, thinking I was asking about his disposition rather than his breed.

"What color is Abelard?" I persisted.

She paused, cocked her head, and smiled, "Mixed."

"Mixed what?" My question came out a bit testy.

She ignored that question and led me into one of the hallways. "There are your three envelopes," she said. They lay on a small, elegantly carved French cherrywood table.

"One for each day you'll be cat sitting next week," Mrs. Salzman explained. She picked up one of the envelopes and opened it—I could see there was a single hundred-dollar bill inside.

My God! Three envelopes! Three hundred-dollar bills! For three visits of about forty-five minutes each to a cat I hadn't even seen yet and might never see! Was this woman mad? It was a truly exorbitant rate of pay. Unless, of course . . . unless there were problems associated with Abelard that she hadn't disclosed.

I was about to ask for a modest reduction in pay when Mrs. Salzman suddenly and dramatically put her finger against her lips, urging silence.

Had she heard Abelard? Was the mysterious cat about to emerge from the shadows?

We waited. Mrs. Salzman closed her eyes and seemed to go into an anticipatory trance. What a strange woman she was: gray hair;

thin, serious face; tall, with a stoop at the shoulders; the very slightest hint of an Austrian accent clinging to her whispers; an abstracted manner as if she was very far away.

We waited. And we waited. And we waited. Where the hell was Abelard?

"Maybe we should call him," I suggested gently.

Mrs. Salzman opened her eyes in horror. I had obviously said the wrong thing.

"He does not like to be called," she said in a compassionate voice, as if, even though I was a professional cat sitter, I was suffering from some kind of mild learning disorder.

"What *does* Abelard like?" I retorted a bit sarcastically.

The sarcasm passed blithely over Mrs. Salzman's head. "He likes flowers and fruit and fresh turkey and music and birds—" She stopped suddenly in the middle of her hysterical list, a bit self-conscious. She smiled and led me to the door, telling me that Abelard wanted more than an employee—he wanted a friend.

I walked home quickly, thinking about *my* cats, Bushy and Pancho.

Granted, they were a bit peculiar. Bushy, the Maine Coon, was, no doubt, one of the drollest beasts ever created. And Pancho, my stray rescued from the ASPCA, well, he was borderline psychotic—spending most of all day and night fleeing from imaginary enemies.

But at least my cats were visible! Not like

Abelard. And my cats obviously had a grudging affection for me.

I climbed the stairs quickly. Thinking about Bushy and Pancho always made me miss them fiercely—even though I had been away from the apartment for less than two hours.

"Alice! You're finally home!"

I stopped suddenly and peered up the badly lit landing, toward the voice.

It was Mrs. Oshrin, my neighbor, the retired schoolteacher.

She was standing at the top of the landing. On either side of her was a very dangerous-looking man.

Kidnappers? Rapists? Junkies? Neighborhood derelicts?

I panicked. I turned sharply on the stairs and started to run back down to seek help.

"Alice!" I heard her call out. "Wait! There's nothing wrong!"

I turned back, confused, still frightened.

"They're police officers, Alice! They want to see you—not me."

I waited, tentative.

"It's all very hush-hush," Mrs. Oshrin pleaded, as if that were an explanation. There was something about the way she used that very old-fashioned phrase—hush-hush"— that sent an anticipatory tingle along my spine. But it wasn't fear.

About the Author

Lydia Adamson is the pseudonym of a well-known mystery writer.